MURDER BY PROXY

MURDER BY PROXY

ROBERT A. BUSCH

iUniverse, Inc.
Bloomington

Murder By Proxy

This is a work of fiction. All of the characters, names, incidents, organizations, and dialogue in this novel are either the products of the author's imagination or are used fictitiously.

iUniverse books may be ordered through booksellers or by contacting:

iUniverse
1663 Liberty Drive
Bloomington, IN 47403
www.iuniverse.com
1-800-Authors (1-800-288-4677)

ISBN: 978-1-4759-2691-0 (sc)
ISBN: 978-1-4759-2763-4 (ebk)

Printed in the United States of America

iUniverse rev. date: 05/21/2012

ONE

Marly Brooks sat gingerly on the edge of her fragile old white wicker chair, the only furniture on the small front porch. Her wide-spaced hazel eyes were focused on the waning fall sun and the eerie glow it cast upon the dwarf palm trees in the front yard of her little cottage. It was really just a small regular house, but it gave her a comforting feeling to think of it as a cottage. True too, it did not have the fabled small white picket fence to close in the front yard; in fact it had no fence at all. There was no need for one because the small yard was barren of flowers or plants; indeed, the weeds had taken over some time ago, burying areas that were once covered with small white stones. One skinny little lemon tree stood gallantly, struggling to survive with only occasional rain water reaching for its thirsty roots; its dry leaves hung pathetically, as if waiting for the end of their life span. Marly had no watering system in place, not even a garden hose connected to an outside spigot.

On the old AM/FM radio balanced precariously on a small unpainted shelf anchored to the wall by her chair, symphonic music played quietly; it had previously presented the Sunday evening news, which included the report that a Doctor Richard Carnes had been murdered early Saturday evening near a convenience market. The report had added that no witnesses to the crime had been identified so far. The police, it was reported, had nothing further to disclose, other than that the shocking crime was under investigation. However, a passerby had told a reporter that he overheard a policeman say that the man had to have been stabbed because of all of the blood on the ground. Marly gave a sigh with a sleight smirk on her face, and said to herself, "Some people in life really get what they deserve; I got what I didn't deserve."

When Marly Brooks had moved into her little house nearly seven years ago she had had great plans in mind to modernize the home, adorn the yards with greenery and flowers, especially Lilacs; she loved sweet smelling Lilacs. Such plans were discarded even before she had had an opportunity to shop for plants and supplies at the J & J Nursery, only a half mile away. She recalled the past events for the thousandth time with a mixture of bitterness and nostalgia, triggered somewhat by the newscast. She had been so proud of herself, being able to buy her first home at only twenty-three, and looking forward to enjoying her little "cottage."

Life had been good back then, what with an enjoyable job at Felix's Camera Shop, and a wonderful boss. Being single hadn't been all that bad, considering that there was hardly a weekend that went by without her having a date on Friday or Saturday night, or both. The customers at the camera shop had given her lots of opportunities to meet young men, and all of them loved to talk to her and they enjoyed her Irish accent, which she had brought with her from Dublin a week after her eighteenth birthday. She reflected back on the thrill of finishing her last year of school and being able to graduate from Orange Grove High School. She recalled what her ambition had been then, to enter the county community college, with the intention of pursuing a business or financial career. And she was finally getting over the depressed feeling she had when she left her mother, dad, older brother and other family members back in Ireland. Marly thought back, once again, about the life she had been enjoying and about the incredible, horrifying turn of events that had followed and which had dashed her plans for a happy future. It wasn't fair . . . it wasn't fair . . . she sobbed.

As she watched the orange-colored sunlight receding over the horizon she thought, "Just like my life, fading away." She closed her watery eyes, as if to block out all of the events that had dramatically, and unhappily, changed her life, just a few years earlier.

Although she was half asleep, she recalled vividly the early morning over six years ago, when she had just finished a breakfast of a scone with cream cheese and some black tea. She had been feeling cheerful and was looking forward eagerly to spending her Sunday morning preparing her garden area for some bright colored Pansies and Petunias, and a Lilac bush. As she washed the last dish from her dinner and put it in the sink rack to dry, the top of her head felt as though she had been stung by a hornet. She let out a yell that would have frightened a Marine, had there been one been nearby. In a moment the intense pain had passed, but she realized that it had to be something other than a hornet sting. But as the day had progressed, Marly's head had again become more painful, to the point where she knew that she could not go to the camera shop on Monday. She was able to reach the owner and manager of the store, Felix Madrone, by phone and explain her plight. He had been very sympathetic, she remembered well, and he had suggested that she might have a migraine headache. He had said, "Marly, it could also be that you have become allergic to something; especially if you have been working in the garden, as you said you were. It could be serious. Let me give you Dr. Carnes' phone number. He is a dermatologist, but if your problem is not up his alley I'm sure that he will know what kind of specialist you should see, and he'll give you the name of a doctor he thinks can treat whatever it is that is causing you such pain. I have been a patient of his for years because of my eczema. He's good."

Marly remembered how she had hesitated at that suggestion, realizing that she had no medical or health insurance, and limited cash. She had said, "I . . . I haven't had to see a doctor since moving here. Is he expensive? Would I have to pay him right away? Maybe I should just take some kind of pain pill right now and see what happens; I have some aspirin. The pain may come back stronger; but at the moment it isn't really too bad; maybe it will just go away."

"No, I don't think that that would be a good idea, Marly," Felix had said sympathetically. "I don't believe that you just have a headache; an aspirin won't fix it I'm sure. Now listen to me," Felix insisted, "I know Doctor Carnes personally. We'll work something out. Now you call him in the morning, after eight; I'll call him at his home tonight and explain your situation to him. Don't worry about coming in late, or not at all tomorrow. Mondays are always pretty slow anyway, but please call me after you see Dr. Carnes, that is if he is able to fit you into his schedule. I would like to know what has caused you that pain, and if you're going to be okay. If you need to have a prescription filled, call me and I'll make some arrangement to get it for you."

Marly remembered feeling so very grateful for having Felix for a boss and had thanked him for being so kind. She called Dr. Carnes' office just after eight on Monday morning, as Felix had suggested; although the doctor was not available to come to the phone, his assistant did talk with him while Marly waited for an answer to her request to see him. Surprisingly, the assistant was able to get an appointment for her with Dr. Carnes at ten o'clock. Marly's thought at the time was that her boss's call to the doctor probably helped her to get an appointment within less than two hours from her call. The assistant instructed her not to take any medication before she came in.

The doctor's nurse assistant took some preliminary information from Marly before she ushered her into an examining room, and Dr. Carnes came in moments later. He proved to be every bit as nice as Felix had indicated, and quickly diagnosed her problem as Shingles, which he explained to her could become quite painful and could be long lasting. "Symptoms vary, however," he had said, "so it is very difficult to predict just how seriously you will be affected, or for how long." He sorrowfully related.

"Shingles! I've never heard of that," Marly had said with a very worried expression, "how could I have gotten it? Is it contagious? It sounds terrible."

The doctor explained the malady to her and the connection to the little red sores that she had developed on the left side of her forehead, but it did not relieve her anxiety or the discomfort she was feeling. He gave her a prescription for a medicine she had never heard of, but he also gave her a shot, explaining that it should ease the pain. It did relieve the pain, but only temporarily, and before the day was over she found it difficult to turn her head, and then she began to have a twitch in her neck. She started to perspire, and wondered what it was that Dr. Carnes had given her. She was afraid to go back to him; she didn't know what to do. It was the only time she saw him, but it was not the last time that she was in pain. She had no idea at the time that the effects of the treatment she had received would last the rest of her life, and that she would almost get sick to her stomach each and every time she would hear the name of Doctor Richard Carnes. The prescription he had given her was not expensive, so she was able to have it filled at the pharmacy herself. The woman pharmacist who discussed the prescribed medication with her was very sympathetic with Marly's condition and suggested that perhaps she should see a neurologist that she thought might help her, and with Marly's agreement, she was able to get an appointment with the neurologist for Marly within the hour.

The doctor's office was not very far away, and Marly was able to walk there in twenty minutes. After filling in some forms and signing some kind of release form, she was taken into an examination room. Dr. Fielder was a no-nonsense doctor who wasted no time in evaluating and discussing her situation. After a few questions and an examination, he stated that she did have an unusual neurological irregularity in her neck, and that it was questionable as to whether surgery would correct the problem. He stated that she had somehow incurred some nerve damage that was difficult to assess. He inquired about her family background, asked about allergies, and learned about the treatment given her by Dr. Carnes, but did not comment on the treatment she had received. He explained to her that an operation would be very expensive, and that there would be no guarantee of success. Since she had not had the condition very long, he suggested that she live with it for awhile with the hope that it would be self-correcting. He said that he felt confident in his evaluation of her condition, but that if she wished, he could recommend another neurologist to give her a second opinion. She was confused at what exactly she should do, but decided to go with the hope that at least the Shingles might disappear by itself. She considered some kind of legal action against Dr. Carnes, but had no idea how to proceed in that direction.

In the discussions that she subsequently had with the one attorney who she thought would help her, he had raised the question of whether she suffered because of an allergic reaction to the prescribed medicine or perhaps a contaminated needle had been used to give her the shot she received for pain. As it turned out, it didn't matter; the lawyer dropped out of the case, claiming that it would be too difficult to substantiate that Dr. Carnes was at fault for her malady, and she was unable to get another lawyer to take her case. The young lawyer that had taken the case on a contingency basis, did send a letter to Dr. Carnes that hinted at a suit, but he dropped the case when he saw that the outcome did not look favorable . . . and that he was not likely to even recover his expenses.

"Why do I keep remembering that horrible time?" she said aloud, coming out of her sorrowful reminiscence, but she couldn't help herself. It was like relating her tragedy to someone else. "I know that whatever it was that he gave me, it had to have been what caused my neck to cramp up and cause this tic or whatever it is that won't let me keep my head up straight. If I had had the money to hire a good lawyer, I could at least have had a better life. Even those lesser known lawyers didn't want my case. Well I wanted Carnes dead for a long time, and now he is." She ended her unhappy reverie and went inside to fix herself a cup of tea; the one thing that always gave her a bit of cheer.

TWO

Anne Whitcomb, nurse and assistant to the murder victim, Doctor Richard P. Carnes, sat at her office station early Monday morning, head down on her folded arms and sobbed. She was too emotionally drained and too tired to even reach for a tissue to dry her dark brown eyes, just letting the tears trickle down on her arms. She was alone and couldn't bring herself to think of what she should do about the patients scheduled for the day, or for the future. The sign she had put on the locked door to the clinic would let today's patients know the facility was closed, but informed them of nothing else. She had heard some of them turn the handle of the door, even though the sign had informed them the office was closed. She couldn't bring herself to go to the door and talk to whoever was there; her emotions held her to her chair.

"How can I tell them that their wonderful and caring doctor was murdered yesterday? My God! If he had just died in some normal way, that would be one thing, but to be murdered!" she exclaimed to herself. "How can that be? Who? Why? And who can I send them to for their problems? What am I supposed to do?!"

Sixteen years ago, Nurse Whitcomb had been a recently widowed thirty-two year old when an employment agency sent her to be interviewed by Dr. Carnes. His assistant had just been married and the newlyweds were to be leaving for Denver in two weeks to open an urgent care center there. Carnes needed an experienced RN to help run his dermatology clinic, and hoped to find someone who could easily and comfortably "connect" with patients of all ages.

At the very first eye contact with the doctor Anne felt at ease, and the interview, though brief, was very pleasant. Issues of working hours, wages, fringe benefits, and all other aspects involved in her employment were settled without any problems. When Dr. Carnes rose from his chair after the interview, he extended his warm hand to Anne and said, "Welcome aboard, Anne; I think that you are exactly what I need to replace Cathy." Anne knew instinctively then that she was going to be happy at the clinic.

Ann was a quick study, and after working only one week with her predecessor, Cathy Ryan, she was happy to hear that Cathy felt confident that Anne was prepared to take over. "She knows your routine, Dr. Carnes," Cathy had told her boss. "She knows everything about the medication, supplies, and the billing procedures." Then she laughingly added, "She even knows how to make coffee the way you like it." The three of them chuckled at that, and Anne was pleased to see the doctor nodding in assent. The departing aide continued, "I'm hoping that you will agree with my assessment of Mrs. Whitcomb, Dr. Carnes, and that for me to be here another week would not be necessary. I really could use more time at home to pack up and get some things shipped to Denver before we leave," she almost pleaded. "I really feel badly about leaving you, you have been wonderful to work for, but I think that you will be happy with Anne."

"From what I have seen," Dr. Carnes had replied, "I have to agree with you." He moved toward the anxious young lady and embraced her as she wiped her teary eyes. "You have done a great job for the years you have been here, Cathy, and yes, you may leave now if you wish. Your final check will be in the mail tomorrow, and it will include next week's pay, plus a little extra send-off thank you." There were happy smiles all around and Cathy left after wishing Anne good luck in her new position.

Anne had worked at the New Grace Hospital in Iowa City after obtaining her RN status, and as often happens when doctors work closely with nurses, she had become attracted to an intern named Bill Whitcomb, and they were married soon after. Anne never liked the snow and cold of Iowa in the winter and they were able to get professional positions in Tampa, Florida. Nearly four years after that Anne quit her job to see if not working would help her conceive, which they had been unable to accomplish up to that time. When that didn't work out they tried in vitro fertilization, even though Bill's sperm had been determined to be very weak. They had previously agreed not to use a donor's sperm, both feeling that there were some psychological problems with that technique. After the second failure with in vitro, they gave up on that method to become parents and started to arrange for an adoption, without either one having any restrictions as to age, sex, or race. They just wished to become parents.

In the midst of arranging for an adoption, Bill had had a fatal heart attack; he was only thirty-five and had been in fairly decent shape for his age. It was devastating to Anne and she mourned deeply for at least three months, hardly leaving the house. The time came however, when it dawned on her that she had to face the reality of it all and get on with her life . . . resigning herself to never becoming a mother. Nursing was going to be her life; to make a totally fresh start, she decided to move to Orange Grove, where a close friend of hers had settled some years before; they had met at the New Grace Hospital.

When she started to work at the clinic, Dr. Carnes was in his middle fifties, gray at the temples, but very physically fit; a trim five-ten or so. After experiencing compatibility and dishonesty problems with two former partners over several years, he had decided to scale back the size of his practice. That made it perfect for Anne, and she felt confident she would be comfortable working for a single physician, a happily married man whose oldest son was about to make him a grandfather, as the doctor had informed her. She had been very happy in her role, until receiving the tragic news of his murder. Now the death of Dr. Carnes has caused her whole world to fall apart.

Suddenly, Anne raised her head from the desk and admonished herself for not calling Mrs. Carnes to see how she was handling the loss of her husband. With only a few years to go before she hit 70, Opal Carnes was still in the athletic body she had enjoyed most of her life. She played tennis three times a week at her club, enjoyed bridge every Thursday at a friend's house, and spent much of her other time at the garden club or in her own garden. One could say that she was a popular person; however, she was not one that could be called a loving person. She did enjoy attention and flattery, almost demanding it. She often picked up a luncheon check for friends with whom she played bridge, as a way of gaining the attention she craved. Particularly self-centered, she only became concerned about anyone else, or anything at all if it interrupted her own schedule of activities. Nor was she the type to play board games in the evening with Dr. Carnes; she was more likely to be reading a book or watching television, while her husband played poker games on his computer, in his den or at one of his favorite casinos.

Anne shook her head, as if that would clear her mind, wiped her eyes, and pushed the programmed number on the office phone for the Carnes' home. She was a bit surprised that Mrs. Carnes answered the phone herself, expecting that one of their two sons would be there, or a daughter-in-law.

"Hi Opal, it's Anne. I'm terribly sorry about Dr. Carnes. I still can't accept the fact that he is gone or what happened to him; it's like a horrible nightmare. It was all I could do this morning to call you; I'm still trying to get myself together. Are you okay?"

"Oh, I'm so glad you called, Anne. Yes, I'm okay, so far, but our two sons are having a tough time. I got the news last night and I came close to fainting; I never expected to lose Richard that way. A heart attack maybe, but murder! Incredible! I can't believe it; it has all happened so fast. Have the police talked to you yet? They were here early this morning, but not for long. I don't know how they could think that I could tell them anything that would help them find out who killed Richard. From what they did say, it seems to have been a robbery. If it was just that, why couldn't they just rob him; it makes no sense to have killed him." Her logic was good, but there was no real emotion.

Anne was amazed at the composure of the doctor's wife, in spite of what she had said, Anne thought that she would at least be as upset as she was herself. She noted that there were no signs of distress in Mrs. Carnes' voice. "The police haven't shown up yet, Opel," Anne replied, "but I'm sure that I'll hear from them soon. Do you have any idea at all as to who could have killed the doctor, or had a reason to do so? I don't have any detailed information about the murder, do you? It doesn't seem possible that it could have been a murder just for someone's wallet, unless the killer was high on meth or something else."

Mrs. Carnes hesitated and Anne thought that she heard a tinkling of ice in a glass, but the new widow responded clearly. "The police said that they could only tell me that he was stabbed right in the heart and that he likely died immediately. They said they could not release any information that might bear on the case, but that there was no denying that the news folks and spectators had publicly stated that robbery was probably the motive because he had just left the nearby convenience food store; not the safest area to be in at nighttime. I can't tell you how many times I told Richard not to go to convenience stores at night; to me it is inviting a problem, but he liked that particular store. He said that the night clerks there were always the most helpful. It was obvious, the police said, that he was walking to his car when it occurred. I imagine that the police have already questioned the store clerk that was on duty last night."

Anne asked Mrs. Carnes, "Do you know if the doctor was carrying much cash? I wouldn't have thought so because he often borrowed small amounts from the office petty cash box for one thing or another. I doubt if he had much on him at all."

"Not much, if any, I'm sure," Opal answered. "He always thought it was foolish to carry a lot of cash. He charged almost everything he spent to one of the two credit cards he carried. I called both of the credit card companies just minutes before you called," she calmly reported. "And of course, I would think that the police have gotten the word out to retail and other businesses to watch for any use of Richard's credit cards. The police did say that his wallet was taken, but for some reason, not his watch; which I don't understand. Why would a robber leave a Rolex watch? Maybe the robber got scared off before he, or she, could grab it."

"That is strange. Well I'm glad that you're alright, Opal, and I'll let you know if anything meaningful comes out of my meeting with the police. Just be calm, it's all in their hands now. Call me if there is anything that I can do for you."

"That will be fine," Opal replied. "I should be alright now, with both of our sons here. I have to rely on you, Anne, to take care of things at the clinic. You know that I never got involved in Richard's business, but I will call our lawyer, Justin Douglas; I think you know him, and I'm sure that he will be in touch with you soon on what should be done with the clinic." They then both ended the call.

Anne sat staring at the phone for awhile, wondering if Mrs. Carnes really cared all that much for her late husband. She knew that the woman's life would not change much with the loss of her mate. She would go on playing tennis and bridge, as usual, and probably would go off on a trip around the world, perhaps searching for a new male to satisfy her other needs. Anne did not believe that money would be a problem for the new widow, whose wealth would in itself be an inducement to any single males that would become aware of her marital status. Too, she recalled overhearing part of a phone conversation not that long ago between her boss and his wife, which she remembered had the tone of some marital problems; so maybe, Anne thought, there was already somebody waiting in the wings. The doctor had been well insured, not to mention his various funds and annuities, which meant that Mrs. Carnes was now part of the "wealthy widows" group. "The hell with worrying about her," Anne said half aloud, "I've got to think of myself . . . again. Damn!"

THREE

It was early Monday afternoon when Senior Detective Beth Reed and her partner Bob Garcia shook Anne Whitcomb out her critical self-assertions when they knocked loudly on the clinic's front door. Anne jumped at the sound and her heart pounded; it was as if she had been awakened in the middle of the night. She quickly realized that the visitor was most likely from the police department; she brushed back her now graying black hair with just her hands, and calmed down enough to slowly rise and unlock the door to the clinic.

"I've been expecting you," she said, perceiving immediately that her expectations were correct, although she was a little surprised that one of the detectives was a woman. She introduced herself: "I'm Anne Whitcomb, Dr. Carnes' assistant," she said, "or at least I used to be," the nurse lamented; her eyes still showed that she had been crying.

"We apologize for not calling to arrange for an appointment with you, Mrs. Whitcomb, but we honestly didn't actually expect that anyone would be here this morning; we just gambled that the clinic would be open. In any event, we're sorry that you lost your employer, Mrs. Whitcomb. From what we have learned, the doctor had a good reputation. We hope to find the killer soon, but we do need help, which is why we are here." the woman detective said. "I am Senior Detective Beth Reed and this is my partner, Detective Bob Garcia." She shook Anne's hand, while Garcia just nodded toward the nervous greeter, but he did hand his card to Anne at the same time that Reed offered her own card to the woman.

Nurse Anne Whitcomb stared down at the cards in her hand as though she was trying to memorize the names; she stood there for a moment, looking pale and unsteady. "If you don't mind, detectives," she said, in almost a whisper, "I've got to get back to my chair and sit down. I'm a bit shaky. I didn't sleep well last night after I got the terrible news about Doctor Carnes." She moved hesitatingly toward her desk and sank heavily into her chair, picking up a clean tissue from the box on her desk to dab at her eyes.

"Of course Mrs. Whitcomb; we understand," Detective Reed assented, as the two visitors took seats on nearby chairs without waiting for any further invitation. They waited quietly until the nurse calmed down enough to speak.

Rousing herself a little, the nurse said, "Please just call me Anne, detectives. You've apparently noticed my wedding ring, but I <u>am</u> a widow, have been for a long time. I left my wedding ring off for awhile after my husband died, but because I found myself being propositioned more times than I cared to be, I went back to wearing the ring. I think that a lot of widows do the same thing. Besides, it's a reminder of the happier times that we had during the time we were together."

"You're right, and that was a smart move, Anne," Detective Garcia confirmed, "It is also actually sort of a safety factor for you as well, because of all of the strangers that you must have had to meet in your capacity. Seeing your ring must have stopped a lot of men cold, before they could even think about being aggressive."

"Well we don't want to waste any more of your time than necessary, Anne," Detective Reed interrupted, "So we better get on with what we need from you that might help us at this early stage in the investigation. Are you feeling well enough to continue discussing the matter, or would you prefer that we give you more time to recover from the shock of the doctor's murder?"

The nurse hesitated for a moment, not really knowing whether or not she felt able to continue, however, she did respond, "I . . . I guess I'm okay," but it was obvious that she did not have it all together.

Detective Reed decided to proceed with the investigation, trying to disregard the nurse's condition; she said, "Right now, Anne, we have no concrete direction to follow, no clue as to who or why this crime was committed. It could still have been just a quick robbery that went tragically awry; however, we do have some reason to believe that there may have been some motive other than robbery involved."

Anne nodded knowingly and replied, "I fully understand, and I want to help you as much as possible, but I don't know how I can do that. This has been a very traumatic event for me, and I'll get myself altogether as soon as possible, but I don't understand why you're saying that there may have been a motive other than robbery for the murder. What other kind of motive would someone have, or who else would have a motive anyway?" She straightened up a bit in her chair, brushed her hair again behind her ears, and asked resignedly, "I guess it doesn't matter anyway, one way or another; I don't care, the doctor is gone; so what would you have me do?"

Detective Beth Reed, a tall and slender woman in her late thirties, appraised the distraught nurse with a critical eye. The hardness often required to be a police woman was evident in her body language and in her poker face, but she softened slightly because of the obviously shocked nurse before her. She quietly said, "We are trying to establish a list of people with whom Dr. Carnes had a contact of one sort or another, so naturally we are interested in his patients. What we are asking, Anne, is for you to review your records and probe your memory as to what patients the doctor has treated over the last two or three years; it is possible that someone may have had some serious conflict with the doctor for one reason or another. There may be one or more persons that were really very angry with the doctor. We believe that among those who harbored deep resentment against the doctor, one of them could have been angry enough to kill him, or have him killed by somebody else."

Detective Bob Garcia interrupted his partner to interject a thought. "Nurse Whitcomb, Anne, the conflict could have been created by any one of a variety of reasons: unsuccessful treatment, the financial charges . . . including any insurance reimbursements, even something you may have done, however unintentionally. From our experiences, Detective Reed's and my own, we also know that we cannot exclude any sexually related cause, such as a husband who may have believed that his wife was violated while being treated by the doctor or who was actually having an affair with him. I think that you can see that we must explore every possibility, regardless as to how strange or sensitive it might be, or even how improbable it might seem to you. We never know from what direction a helpful clue may come."

"That is absolutely correct, Bob; you covered the point well," Beth Reed confirmed. "We rarely have a clue that falls out of the sky; we usually have to dig them out; we are just starting to dig and we think that this is a good place to start. Now, Anne, do the names of any troublesome patients come to your mind at this moment, or do you need more time to think about it? At the same time, we don't want to exclude anyone else, such as a supplier, salesperson, or even a friend that may have had some serious unpleasantness with the doctor. We cannot limit our investigation of any individuals at this time that may have had an altercation with the doctor, for whatever reason."

Nurse Whitcomb rolled her wide eyes upward, as though she might see a patient's name or face on the office ceiling, but in a second or two she gazed back at her interrogators and answered: "I . . . I'm sorry detectives, my mind just can't focus on anything right now. I'm just drawing a blank. Frankly, I'm also worried about all of the people who have been trying to call me; I took the phone off of the cradle before you arrived because I didn't think that you would appreciate that interruption; I'm feeling guilty about that now because some of them are almost like friends; I've known many of them for so long that we are on a first name basis. My brain is in a whirl right now, but if I can get a good night's rest tonight maybe my brain will function a little better tomorrow."

Detective Reed appeared to be unhappy with the response, but she accepted the fact that Nurse Anne Whitcomb was unable to instantly generate any helpful information. It was obvious to both detectives that the nurse had experienced a traumatic event, one which affected her deeply. Reed decided to grant the nurse more time to recall any past unpleasantness with any patient. "We will leave you then, for now Anne, but you have my card. In the event that you do recall the names of anyone who had an unpleasant confrontation with the doctor, please call me. It would seem more logical though, that you might find the names of the troublesome patients easier by reviewing your files, rather than by racking your brain. I would think that it would be necessary to go back over only the last two or three years in your files; unless you know of some reason to go back further. A name, or even two, may eventually stand out in your records, or in your mind. It's very possible, of course, that you might not uncover any bitter patients at all, but if you do, call us as soon as you can. Whether you turn up any names or not, please call us so that we can move on to other prospects." The detectives left after a brief goodbye, but neither had any confidence that the nurse was going to be helpful. Besides, it also didn't seem reasonable to them that an unhappy patient could be angry enough to murder their doctor, but then murder cases were usually full of surprises.

FOUR

On the south side of Orange Grove, Zach Segal was just starting to read the Tuesday morning edition of the Wall Street Journal while enjoying the coffee he had purchased at the Blue Fin Deli next door to his antique shop, the "Auld Lang Syne." He normally never opened the front door to the store until ten o'clock, and it was only nine-thirty, so he expected to be able to enjoy his coffee and paper for the next half hour. After taking a sip of his coffee, he opened up the Journal and started to read, but he heard a noise at the door, looked up and recognized that a recently new customer was at the front door attempting to enter. He cursed himself for having turned on the front lights, but at the same time decided that his coffee and paper could wait; money was more important.

Zach rose, put his coffee cup and paper on the counter in front of him, went to the door, unlocked it, and greeted his customer as she entered. "I'm surprised to see you again so soon, Mrs . . . ,"

"Gordon," the customer reminded Zach, smiling graciously. "Elizabeth Gordon."

"Oh yes, thank you. I'm much better at remembering faces than I am with names; sorry. Is there a problem with that cream and sugar set you bought last Saturday?" he asked.

"Not at all Zach," Mrs. Gordon answered, "it just struck me when I returned home that I really should have purchased a little cookie plate that would go with the cream and sugar set. I'm in a new bridge group and I was informed that whoever is the hostess for the week only serves small cookies, crackers, or candies, and of course, coffee. No lunch or heavy hors d'oeuvres. I see that you were trying to enjoy your morning coffee while reading your paper, so don't bother with me. If you don't mind, I'll just browse around the shop and maybe I'll find exactly what I need."

"That's fine; take your time, Mrs. Gordon. I think that the best area to look would be the china collection group almost at the back of the shop," Zach suggested, as he pointed her toward the rear of the shop. "Call for me if you need help. I'll be here finishing my coffee and paper, and thank you for allowing me to do so."

"You're quite welcome," Mrs. Gordon answered as she walked down the small aisle way leading toward the rear of the shop.

The telephone rang at that moment and Zach picked it up and answered by merely giving the caller the shop's name, shortened to just "Auld Lang."

"Hi Zach, it's Sam Meyers. Are you busy, or can you talk for a minute?"

"It's okay, Sammy, good to hear from you again, its' been awhile; I opened up early for a customer, but she's in the back of the shop right now; I should have five minutes or so. What's up?"

"Have you read the papers lately, Zach, or listened to the news? There's a hot bit of published news that should be of interest to you," Sammy answered.

Zach put down the coffee he had in his left hand and replied, "No, I haven't paid any attention to the news at all, Sammy, until just now that is. I was just starting to read the Wall Street Journal when that customer came to the door. I didn't even pick up the local paper yesterday or this morning. I've been busy with other things. Did I miss something important?"

"Well you should be happy to hear that your least favorite dermatologist, Dr. Carnes was murdered last night. They said that he was stabbed right in the heart," Sammy informed his friend. "He had just left a convenience market and apparently was about to get into his car; they think that it was a robbery. Funny thing, though, the robber, or killer, just took his wallet, but left his expensive Rolex watch. It looks like maybe he was interrupted and just took off. A little stupid, I think; hell, the wallet might not have had any cash in it at all, while the watch was probably worth a few thousand, even in the underground. He'll be lucky if he gets to use any of the credit cards, and he'd actually be smart not to even try, not with the way the police can trace charge slips nowadays."

Zach held the phone in his right hand and was silent for a moment, as though he was contemplating how he would answer his friend. "No, I didn't hear that news, but as you know, I can only be happy that it happened. Remember, he screwed me out of $15,000; how could I not be happier than a Muslin martyr with 70 virgins tending to my needs?" They both laughed at the expression.

"Why don't we get together for lunch or dinner soon; I think that I have an idea as to how you might recover some, if not all of your fifteen grand from the doc's wife, or maybe from one of your rich bitch customers, and maybe a little bonus at the same time," Sammy suggested. "From what you have told me in the past the widow lady is a bit of a flake, probably has no idea of the value of some of the antiques or jewelry in her home. Old doc was the one who probably bought all of her jewelry anyway; the only problem I see with her might be that she has too damn much jewelry already. I have heard though, that a lot of women believe that there is no such thing as having too much jewelry. I think that you once joked about her dripping with gold and diamonds, but she still might bite on the plan that I have in mind, which I think is a "gem" of a plan."

"You've got a good memory, Sam, and what I told you previously about her jewelry has stuck in your mind. Apparently that is what you want to talk about. If you have some kind of scheme involving Mrs. Carnes' jewelry, I would be happy to team up with you on a plan that would recover even just some of my loss. I am definitely interested in what you have in mind. Let me call you back to set up a meeting, maybe lunch at Rubio's tomorrow. I've got to hang up now; the one customer in the shop is heading my way. I'll talk to you later, Sam." He hung up the phone just as Mrs. Gordon returned to the front of the store with something in her hand.

"I'll take these two plates, Zach; they match, and I'm sure that I can use both of them; they are perfect for what I need; I got lucky," the lady customer said, very pleased with having found what she wanted.

"I'm glad that you found what would work for you, Mrs. Gordon," Zach replied. He was pleased that she paid in cash, and he thanked her for coming in again. Then he had another thought, a bit of inspiration, having recognized from the way she was dressed, and her demeanor, that she was a woman who benefited from a high level of income. "I don't know if you would ever be interested in buying anymore jewelry, Mrs. Gordon; you probably have all you need or want. But in this business I have opportunities from time to time to purchase really good jewelry through people who sell off estate assets, and the prices are very attractive. Do you think that you might be interested if I were to receive some high-end pieces? As you can tell from the shop inventory, I normally do not handle any contemporary jewelry, but I make exceptions." He paused for a moment to gauge Mrs. Gordon's reaction to his proposal.

She smiled at him and said, "As a matter of fact, Zach, personally I do have just about all of the jewelry that I'll ever need, but I have been thinking about our two daughters, who by coincidence, were married ten years ago on almost the same day. I have thought about buying something unique for each of them when they celebrate their anniversaries, which will be next month. To answer your question, yes I might be interested. If you will let me know when something good comes in, I would appreciate having the opportunity to evaluate what pieces you would have available. As I mentioned, however, I don't have a lot of time to make some kind of purchase. Unless you can come up with something fairly soon I'll have to shop for some other kind of gift. As I said, the celebrations are not far off. Give me a slip of paper and a pen or pencil; I'll give you my number so you can call me if something good comes in, but please don't give the number to anyone else, it's unlisted. I don't believe that you know that my husband is State Representative Webb Gordon, and he doesn't want everybody and his brother to be calling us. We get too many phone calls now, especially at the dinner hour, so Webb would be unhappy to receive any more."

Zach was pleased to hear the acceptance of his suggestion and promised to call his customer if he had some attractive pieces come in. As she started toward the door he politely said, "Tell your husband that I think that he's doing a great job, and thanks for coming in again, Mrs. Gordon. I promise to keep your number confidential, and I will remember your name from now on." she laughed as she exited the shop.

Zach stood there, looking after his customer and wondering about how they could work out a scam that she would fall for. He decided that he should call Sam and clue him in on what he had discussed with Mrs. Gordon. He was sure that Sam would have some thoughts on how to proceed, and let him know he thought he might have a "pigeon" ready to be plucked. Although it was still early in the day, Zach felt like celebrating. He stepped away from the counter and went to the other side of the partition that shielded his desk area. He reached down and pulled open his lower left drawer, retrieved a half-empty bottle of Jack Daniels and a shot glass, which he quickly filled with the bourbon. Before he downed the beverage, he raised the glass and said with a laugh, "Here's to you, Mrs. Gordon, may you become my best customer." He started to recap the bottle, hesitated, and then said, "Oh hell, you can't walk on one leg," and then poured himself another shot.

FIVE

It was Tuesday afternoon, just a day after the detectives Beth Reed and Bob Garcia had met with Nurse Anne Whitcomb, and the two were in a conference room at headquarters discussing what they thought should be the next step in their investigation of the "convenience store murder," which it had become known as in the office. They were distracted when Beth Reed's cell phone tinkled; she answered quickly, "Reed here." It was Anne Whitcomb.

"This is Anne Whitcomb, detective. Would it be possible for us to meet soon, detective, maybe this afternoon?" Anne asked. "I have some information for you that may or may not be helpful, but it would take too much time to give it to you over the phone, and you will probably want to make some notes or tape the data I have for you. I am anxious to give you whatever you need so I can get back to clearing up some of the paperwork that has piled up on my desk. I also have some questions that you might answer to satisfy my curiosity, or have you already solved the mystery as to who killed Dr. Carnes?"

Reed was pleased that Anne had called back so soon, and was eager to meet with the nurse, but she laughed at Anne's question. "No, I wish that I could say that we have solved the case, and I'm sorry to say that we haven't made much progress on the crime so far,

Anne. Actually, we're hoping that we can use some of the information that you have to steer us in the right direction. We are both available now, so we will be very happy to meet with you at the clinic; how about if we meet you there in about half an hour?" "That would be perfect; I'm here now," Nurse Ann agreed. "I'm anxious to get this out of the way so I can begin to work with Mrs. Carnes and her lawyer to settle all of the problems involved with closing up the clinic for good, or turning it over to another dermatologist, which is what I'm hoping will happen. About all that I have been able to do since Monday has been to make calls to patients or respond to the umpteen incoming calls from them, suppliers, insurance companies, stock brokers, and the agency handling the leasing of this office. Fortunately, the traffic in the door here has not been too bad, so I'm keeping the door unlocked for now, so please just come on in."

"Good," Detective Reed responded; "Detective Garcia and I will pick up some hot coffee for us on the way over. See you soon."

When the detectives arrived they found Nurse Anne Whitcomb examining a pile of files on her desk, she looked composed and attractive. She was dressed in blue jeans and a white short-sleeved top. Her hair was tied at the back, more like a pony tail than a bun. And although she wore little makeup, her slight build and her attire gave her a more youthful appearance. It also helped that she had not been crying, as she had been before their first meeting, and her eyes were bright and clear.

The two detectives walked in briskly, with Garcia carrying a paper bag with three cups of coffee. "Hello again, Anne," Beth Reed started, "Bob has the coffee, and we brought sweetener and creamer, if you need it." As she talked, Detective Garcia passed around the coffee, and the partners took seats in the two conference chairs in front of the nurse's desk. The situation was much more comfortable than their first meeting, and the detectives were hoping that this time some more meaningful information would be obtained from the nurse/assistant.

"Thank you; this is just the kind of pick-up I needed," Anne said, as she took a slow sip of her coffee. I have been so eager to get this patient file review over with that I didn't even bother to make any this morning. I had always made coffee for the office as soon as

I would come in because Dr. Carnes was a coffee junkie; we always had a pot brewing. Even if he had had coffee at home, he didn't do any work here until he got a full mug in his hand. He was kind of a slow starter; we never took any patients before eight thirty; he liked to stand around for a few minutes and talk about the weather, politics, or almost anything. Anyway, I just got right into the files this morning because I knew that I would have to have everything in shape before meeting again with you two. As I think I said, I also have to have everything ready for a meeting, which I'm not looking forward to, with Mr. Justin Douglas, Dr. Carnes' lawyer. Maybe it's just me, but my past experience with the man has not been very pleasant; more like the opposite. After our very first meeting, I discovered that he was not the nicest person to work with. I imagine that you will have to meet with Mr. Douglas sometime; be prepared to have an unpleasant experience; although I would expect him to be a little nicer with you guys."

"Well we may eventually have to meet with him, Anne, but at this point, however, he is not in the picture, but who knows? I'm glad you like the coffee, Anne, and I don't want to rush you, but have you had any luck at all, in digging up some suspects for us, or have all of the doctor's patients been pleasant to work with?" Detective Reed asked.

"Hardly . . . that would be a miracle," Anne responded. "I don't think that any doctor, or anyone in business could ever say that; people are people. Dr. Carnes practice was pretty normal, and over the sixteen years that I have worked here, we have had our share of complainers, with or without cause. As a matter of fact, in the years that I have been in nursing I would guess that 95% of the patients that I have met have never created a problem. The majority of them are almost a joy to work with. It's the other five percent that create difficulties of one sort or another; some real, some imagined. I believe that other businesses serving the public have pretty much the same experience, but you know that I'm sure." She stopped talking for a minute while she enjoyed a bit more of her coffee; the detectives were patient with her and sat quietly waiting for her to continue, enjoying their own coffee.

Anne apologized for the deviation: "I'm sorry for straying from your reason for being here detectives. Anyway, to answer your question, I did find that three of our former patients stand out because of problems they had with Dr. Carnes, and none of them remained as patients after the problems caused them to stop being treated here. I must admit though, that in at least one of the cases, the doctor may have asked that they not return." Anne stopped, as though she expected to be interrupted, but continued when there were no questions. However, both detectives had taken out small shorthand-type writing pads and were making notes; they had earlier decided against taping Nurse Whitcomb's report, wanting her to feel more at ease to talk freely.

The nurse sipped her coffee and seemed eager to continue reporting; she said, "The saddest case that created a serious rift with the doctor involved a single woman who had come from Ireland some years before and who had no family here. She came in with a really bad case of Shingles and was treated by the doctor. A friend of his, a Felix Madrone, had referred her to Dr. Carnes. She was a sales clerk in the camera shop owned by Mr. Madrone; I don't have the name of the shop in my files. As I remember it, though, there was some kind of arrangement for the doctor's fee; I think that it was sort of a charity case, or her employer paid some part of her bill. I know that the doctor gave her some oral medication, free, for the pain, and a shot of some kind. The doctor later concluded that she must have had an allergic reaction to one or both things because she quickly developed a permanent tic or restriction to the movement of her head, which I believe began after she returned home. She came back in the very next day according to the records, and Dr. Carnes told her that he could not treat that development, but that he really thought something other than his medication caused the problem. I believe that he told her that he thought that it was possibly an allergic reaction to the medication, and that he expected that it would clear up naturally. Trying to be helpful, he did give her the names of several specialists that he thought would be able to help her if the condition persisted. We didn't know what happened with her until about a month or so later when Dr. Carnes received a letter from a lawyer that indicated that his client, Marly Brooks, intended to sue. I recall the doctor muttering about his trying to settle the claim out of court, but I never heard any specific amount mentioned. We never heard from the lawyer again, and nothing ever happened. I don't know if she is even alive, but the doctor was never sued, as far as I know. I think that Dr. Carnes checked with the state bar after he got the letter, and learned that the attorney hired by Miss Brooks, had been at that time, just recently admitted. I suspect that he probably wasn't getting paid, and couldn't afford to do pro bona work." Anne stopped talking and finished drinking the rest of her coffee. "Could she be a suspect?" she asked. "She was awfully young; I can't think of her as being capable of murder."

"However, that does all sound as though she at least had a motive for some kind of revenge," Detective Garcia responded. "If what you told us is the truth, and I'm sure that it is, then surely she would be bitter. That bitterness could have been festering for the past years, to the point where she wanted to finally put an end to it. Of course we'll have to conduct an investigation of her before we draw any conclusions. She could also have a perfect alibi for last Saturday night. On the other hand, we cannot discount the alternative for her, that of paying someone else to do the deed for her. She is definitely more than just a party of interest in this case. Do you agree, Beth?" Garcia asked his partner.

"That does sound like Miss Brooks had a motive," Detective Reed said, "but whether it could justify murder is another thing. Miss Brooks might still be angry, if she is alive, but how angry depends to some extent on her personality, and what kind of life she has had since that incident. She may be the timid type; then again she might be capable of harboring deep seated hatred that could generate a violent action. Please write down her name, address and phone number you have, and any other information that we can follow up on. You might include the name and any other information you have on Mr. Madrone, Miss Marly's employer at the time. We'll take that with us when we leave, along with any other information on the other two patients that you know had some serious disagreements with the doctor."

"Now then, Anne, what about the other two problem patients?" Detective Garcia asked. He put aside, at least for the moment, a flashing thought that it might be possible that Nurse Whitcomb had not included the name of someone in her list of possible suspects because of some personal reason. He had had prior experience with witnesses who, for one reason or another, withheld important information until they were forced to reveal it. He made a mental note to discuss that possibility with his partner later, when they would be evaluating the information of the three persons she had selected.

"There was a Zach Segal who had been a patient for quite awhile," Anne responded to Detective Garcia's question, "He suffered from chronic athlete's foot, which is really a form of Herpes. I never felt that he was very clean and that didn't help him in trying to get rid of the ailment. After he had been a patient for quite awhile He talked Dr. Carnes into some kind of financial investment. I never knew anything specific about it, but from what I remember, a fair amount of money was involved. Then one day Mr. Segal came storming in here madder than hell and he and the doctor had a pretty violent argument. He never came in again after that, but he and Dr. Carnes talked frequently on the phone, unpleasantly. It was obvious that both men were very unhappy with each other over one of the investments they had had together. I have written down his name, address, and the phone number that we had in the file for you, including the name and address of the antique shop he owns, the "Auld Lang Syne; an odd name, but one that is easy to remember." Unless the shop is closed I would suspect that that's where you will most likely find him. I think that the business is just a one-person operation."

Detective Reed reacted favorably to that information and said, "That individual may be more of a suspect than Miss Brooks. As a male, he would be more likely to take out his vengeance in a violent way, and be more apt to use a knife."

"Why is that?" Anne asked, a bit surprised at hearing that remark, and looked at Detective Reed in some amazement.

"As I'm sure you would know, a knife draws blood quickly, the wielder must be very close to the victim to commit the crime, and could easily get splattered with blood, which would really bother a lot of women, even one that might be a killer. And it could require some hand strength, depending on the size and power of the victim and the criminal," Reed answered. "Historically, murders committed by females have been accomplished either by poison or by gunshot, not with a knife. Admittedly, that has been changing of recent times, but they are still the manners favored by women. Many hardened criminals know, incidentally, that a knife is a bit harder for us to trace after a crime; it is a silent weapon, it can be more easily disposed of, or if found, may be difficult to tie to the crime. There are no shells to match to a gun, no serial numbers to be traced, whereas a knife can be wiped or washed clean and be restored to its normal storage place, nesting in a kitchen drawer along with a lot of other knives, and," she chuckled, "it won't go off accidentally."

Detective Bob Garcia picked up the interrogation, "I believe that you said, Anne, that you found the names of three patients that could be suspects?"

"Yes, I did detective, but I don't have much behind my suspicions to really justify putting the third one, Mr. Roland LeBland, in that category. He was more of a gentleman, more business-like than Mr. Segal; certainly better groomed. He was a patient for only a short time, and he merely had a rash on both forearms, although it did cause some severe itching. Dr. Carnes had quickly diagnosed his problem as being from the bites of pine tree mites, which are not common in this part of the country, so he must have been traveling up north. Dr. Carnes said that he must have had sort of an allergic reaction to the bites because he complained of considerable discomfort right after the rash became inflamed. The doctor gave him something to immediately reduce the discomfort and also a prescription for something that would take care of the problem. I believe that Mr. LeBland was a realtor or commercial building salesperson. The best that I can recall from the bits of conversation that I did hear back then, it seems that Dr. Carnes had agreed to buy a small building with Mr. LeBland, but there was some kind of flaw in the paperwork and the doctor reneged on paying for his half interest in the property. Apparently there was a substantial deposit that Mr. LeBland had put up for the doctor, as a matter of convenience, but it was lost because it was not recoverable if the deal fell through. Dr. Carnes felt that it was not his fault, and that LeBland should have known better. I always believed that Dr. Carnes was a really fine doctor and that he was honest, but I must admit that he did seem to get into some awkward business situations from time to time. I know that soon after I started working for him, he invested in a launderette and dry-cleaning operation that failed, but that didn't cause any other problems. He also often went to casinos on the east coast, and even to Las Vegas, but I think that he also liked to take gambles in financial investments. Here is the business card that Mr. LeBland gave me when he came in for the first time; I won't need it anymore, I'm sure. The company is the A to Z Commercial Properties." Anne said as she handed the card to Detective Reed. "I believe that the company is still operating because the name of the company was in the papers just recently because a former partner had filed for bankruptcy relief."

"Well Anne, I think that you did a great job, you've given us something to work on, whether or not any of these leads pan out. Don't you agree Bob?"

"Yes, of course. Miss Whitcomb, Anne. we appreciate the time and trouble you took to dig these names out of your files," Detective Garcia acknowledged. "I'm sure that you are aware of the possibility that if any one of these suspects prove to be involved in the doctor's murder that we will need to have you in court to confirm some of the information that you have given us. Because of that possibility, it is important that you keep us informed if you plan to be away for awhile, take a position with another clinic, or move your residence. You understand that it may be necessary for us to contact you at short notice, so we have to be able to reach you."

"Yes," Anne agreed, "I understand. I have never had a reason to be in a court, so in a way I would not relish the experience of testifying, but I would do it gladly if it resulted in putting the doctor's killer away for life, or ending his. Even if it does turn out to be just a robbery; it seems so stupid to end someone's life over cash or credit cards. Maybe the killer was high on drugs or was stupid drunk. I even wonder if somehow it could have been a case of mistaken identity; maybe it was supposed to be an intentional killing of somebody else, but whoever did it made a mistake."

"We may never know about that, Anne, but it's always a possibility; you may have given us another twist to think about it this case," Reed responded as the two detectives rose from their chairs. Beth Reed extended her hand to thank Anne for her work; Garcia nodded to her as well, in recognition of what she had been able to furnish the team. Reed added: "If needed, we'll call on you again, Anne, if not, then you will know that we were successful in following other leads. If that does happen, we will make sure that someone contacts you from our office to let you know." The two detectives exited the clinic with a wave and Anne sat back in her chair, let out a soft sigh, and said to herself, "Now what the devil should I be doing?" Before she could ponder that question any further, the telephone rang.

The caller was Mr. Justin Douglas, the lawyer for Mrs. Carnes; without much of a greeting, he just quickly introduced himself over the phone, even though they had met before, and he then requested that he would like to meet with Anne as soon as possible, whenever she would be available, but his manner indicated that he expected her to be able to meet him quite soon. Having had some unpleasantness with the man in the past she was not looking forward to working with him; however, she realized that there were things to be done with him, and she also felt that she was not in a position to refuse his request. Anne reluctantly agreed to meet Mr. Douglas at the clinic at nine o'clock the following morning. As Anne expected, the phone conversation was brief; the man was not one to spend time with chit-chat, even serious chit-chat. She started preparing herself mentally, thinking about how she could make the self-centered man understand her position, and possibly also have him be of some assistance to her, career-wise. She thought, for just a second or two, about the possibility that Mr. Douglas might turn the legal work required over to a junior member of his firm, someone she might enjoy working with a bit more than Douglas himself. "I'm dreaming," she said to herself.

SIX

As the two detectives entered their car after their session with Nurse Anne, the senior detective, Beth Reed, said to her partner, "You know that idea that Anne Whitcomb came up with may not be too far-fetched, Bob; to be honest, I never gave that possibility a thought. That would make this case just as hard to solve as it would if it were a random killing. I think that we should go back to headquarters and meet with our chief, Clyde Hopson, before we go any further, Bob. You and I have to review our notes anyway, at least to see if we agree as to which is the best lead to follow first; then we can talk to Hopson. Even if we don't agree at the moment, I think it would be best if we settled that point before we meet with Hopson; you know, to present a united front." They both chuckled at that.

Garcia nodded in agreement; "But I would hope that he would also have some information on what the team that examined the crime scene may have found that would help us, if anything." Garcia stated. "Maybe the killing was, after all, just a robbery, but it was the most violent one that I've ever heard of. It's so odd, Beth; I was only involved in a couple of murders before we joined up, and from almost the very beginning in every case it wasn't very long before we knew why it had taken place. In this case we are struggling to determine the motive as well as trying to find the killer; we have everything from a random murder, to embittered patients of the doctor, to a possibility of it being a case of mistaken identity. I hope that we can keep our sanity."

"If it was really a robbery that just got botched," Beth Reed interjected, "why did the robber just take the victim's wallet, but left his watch? It had to be because he was interrupted, but then why wouldn't there have been a witness? It's reasonable, I think, to presume that some person could have been just walking by or a car had just driven up. If there was no witness or interruption, why didn't the killer take the watch? We know that it was a Rolex, and without question it had to have been worth a lot more than what was in the victim's wallet. It might go down as the dumbest robbery ever. The fact that the killer did take the doctor's wallet makes me believe that the mistaken identity scenario is less credible. In that situation, I doubt if the killer would stop to take the victim's wallet. Let's hope that Hopson has some answers for us." Reed concluded as they drove into the headquarters' parking area.

Before they settled into chairs in one of the vacant conference rooms, each poured themselves a cup of coffee from the coffee station. As they pulled out their notes, Bob Garcia was the first to venture an opinion: "I have really struggled to arrive at the most likely culprit, Beth, but I think that it looks like the woman, Marly Brooks. As I see it, she shapes up as having had the best motive for murdering the doctor; not doing it herself, but having somebody else do it for her. I lean toward her having a surrogate; it just doesn't seem realistic that a woman would stab someone to death. We know that in cases where a woman does stab someone, it usually involves excessive alcohol consumption at a party or during a violent family argument; that kind of action often escalates into a self defense situation. Premeditation is something else. As to Miss Marly, in the first place she would have a transportation and execution problem because of her physical condition. What do you think, Beth; do you think that she is capable of a pre-meditated murder, or to have someone else do it or her? Or am I way off the mark?"

"Well, Bob, personally I lean toward following our antique shop owner first; it would seem logical that he might have more of the type of personality that could become violent. What bothers me most about considering him as a suspect is what might have been his motive; it seems to me that the amount of money lost in his case is too insignificant to justify murder. On the other hand, if he has a big ego, or considers the loss to have been an affront to him as a businessman, he may have been festering the resentment until he felt that he had to do something about it. Then too, we don't have enough information on the man to know if he is a user, or if in some other way his mental capacity has been affected. Hopson will undoubtedly have another opinion, but I'll bet he'll give us the freedom to pick the lead we want to follow first. If he does, and you agree, I'd like to get Brooks out of the way, which is what I think that you want to do in the first place. If we clear her, we can then concentrate on the other two possible suspects. Let's go meet with the boss."

Garcia was pleased that his partner wanted to pursue the Brooks lead first. They left the conference room together and walked down the hall to Hopson's office, hoping that their boss would be able to give them some confirmation of the direction they had considered to follow.

Chief Clyde Hopson looked up from the papers before him as he heard his office door open; he stood up and greeted each of the detectives with a handshake. "Glad you guys came in now," he said, "Right now I'm a little pressed for time. I've got a meeting with the DA on another case in ten minutes, but let me hear what you've got on the Carnes murder. Sit down."

Senior Detective Reed described the results that she and Garcia had as the consequence of meeting with Anne Whitcomb. Hopson listened carefully; he seemed pleased to learn of the leads that had developed, then turned to Detective Garcia, and asked, "Anything to add to that, Bob?"

"No sir, I think that Beth gave you the whole picture. The only difference of opinion that we have is just which suspect we should zero in on first, even though at this point we agree that there is no one obvious lead to follow. Then we have also wondered if the original crime scene investigators had come up with anything that would point us in another direction, or add to what we already know about the physical evidence generated. We're still up in the air in terms of knowing whether the murder was the result of a robbery gone bad or if it was a vengeance crime for one reason or another. Obviously if it was to have been a robbery, and the murder purely a random act, it will be a lot more difficult to solve." Both detectives waited silently while their superior reflected on their comments.

Chief Hopson rubbed his balding head, played "cradle" with his two hands for a few moments, brushed his mustache with his fingers, and then spoke quickly. "I wish that I had more time to give to this crime right now guys, but I don't, so I'm going to throw it back on your laps. I hate doing that, but unfortunately we've got seven homicides going now, including a double. We're all pressed for time. The original crime scene investigators on the Carne's murder haven't come up with anything except the report given by the evening clerk at the convenience market. There were no other witnesses to question, at least none that would step forward and be identified. All that the clerk, who was a man, could tell the boys was what he saw from inside the store as he followed the victim out the door with his eyes, which he said is his and the managements' normal safety precaution for night customers. He had stated to the investigators that there appeared to be another man of medium height and build getting out of his car as Dr. Carnes was unlocking his own vehicle. But he also said that he had been distracted just at that moment by the phone, which he turned to answer. When he hung up and then looked outside again, he didn't see anyone standing in the parking area. Concerned because he saw that the victim's car was still there; he said that he just felt that something was wrong, so he decided to call the police. He never went outside to see what had happened, even after the police were there, which he again said was following company rules. That still leaves us with the mystery as what kind of crime was committed. I do think that you should question that clerk again; maybe he will recall something else that would help us." He rose from his chair and apologetically said, "I gotta get going, sorry, but keep plugging guys; we've got to get this bastard, no matter what his motive might have been. The doctor was well known, not just a nobody; we may get some publicity that we don't want on this one. Oh, one more item, almost forgot. One of the news' guys that hangs around here looking for stories, talked to the receptionist; I think Cindy was on the desk at the time. He had read about the murder of Dr. Carnes and said to Cindy that he wondered if it had anything to do with Mrs. Carnes filing for divorce. I don't know how he found out about that. It may or may not be important. Maybe that divorce filing has been in the works for quite awhile; if it happened recently, you may have another lead to follow. You will want to talk to him, for sure; Cindy can give you his name. You never know, there could be a connection." He rose and gave a brief hand wave as he went out the door in a hurry.

"Well that news was a bit of a shocker, Bob," Detective Reed addressed her partner; "Mrs. Carnes filing for divorce just before her husband is murdered; quite a coincidence, if that was what it was. Realistically though, I would be surprised if it develops into anything that will help us to solve the crime. We'll have to investigate Mrs. Carnes as a matter of routine anyway; I hope that I'm wrong, seeing it as just another unproductive use of our time," Beth Reed said, "but we should talk to Cindy first. I feel confident that Nurse Whitcomb didn't know about that either; she would surely have told us. We should check that out later; the divorce papers that have been filed would not likely hint that Mrs. Carnes did have a motive for murder; that does not mean, however, that she may not have had one. At the moment, though, let's go visit our Miss Brooks, as we planned, after we see Cindy about that reporter.

The team stopped by the receptionist's desk and was pleased to see that Cindy was on duty. Detective Reed asked her if she had any detailed information that she might have in regard to the facts or the hearsay on the filing of divorce papers by Mrs. Richard Carnes. Cindy said, "Well you guys know as well as I do that reporters are always looking at criminal and legal filings of any sort so they can have something to write about. In this case one of them just picked up on the name because of the Carnes murder being reported in the papers. He did tell me that he had caught the word "incompatibility" when he glanced through the papers that were filed at the court handling all divorce cases in this county. That's about all I can tell you about that, but if you want to call the reporter, I have his card. I told him who you were, gave him both of your names and advised him that one of you would probably call him today."

"Hold unto that card, Cindy," Detective Reed directed, "We may ask for it later. Right now Bob and I hope to meet with Marly Brooks, the woman who could well be at the root of this murder case. Should anyone ask, we probably won't be able to make it back this afternoon." She turned to her partner and said, "Bob, while you drive I'll see if I can get her on my cell phone and get the okay to come and have a little visit. I would love to get this case solved, but I almost wish that we don't find her to be the guilty party."

"I know, Beth, I feel the same way," Detective Garcia agreed. I'll bring in the tape recorder; for some reason I feel that we may want to replay the session. It might be necessary if she has any difficulty speaking clearly because of the condition of her neck. We can always stop recording anytime that you think that she is going nowhere as a suspect, or if we feel that she is uncomfortable knowing that what she says is being recorded."

"That's a good idea, Bob," Beth Reed said, "then we can skip the note taking, which I hate to do anyway; my notes are always difficult to read back. Should the recording session prove fruitful, if we do it, it would be necessary to maintain the tape for later confirmation of her statements. I've got her phone ringing, but she doesn't answer. She may be out, is sleeping or otherwise indisposed, or just sitting on her little porch and can't hear the phone. Maybe she just doesn't want to answer the phone. Keep driving, Bob; with her condition, I suspect that she will be available when we get there."

SEVEN

Marly Brooks was there when they arrived, sitting in her little wicker chair on the front porch, seemingly not looking at anything in particular. Her little radio was tuned to an FM station, which quietly played some symphonic selection. She was dressed in a casual housecoat and slippers, her every day, stay-at-home outfit. Her hazel eyes were clear and bright; her auburn hair was cut short and pulled back behind her ears, held in place with small clips. She showed no excitement when the team introduced themselves, and she quietly invited them into the house and directed them to straight chairs around the kitchen table. It was disturbing to the detectives to see her unable to keep her head in a normal position, and the slight tic on the left side of her neck was distracting. Otherwise, however, she seemed to have no other physical impairment. She was slender, but well proportioned, only a bit on the pale side. She did become a little disturbed when Detective Garcia set up and turned on the recorder and then explained their reasons for the visit. Senior Detective Reed, quickly aware of Marly's discomfort with the recorder, asked her partner to shut off the recorder, and then further clarified why it was necessary for them to question several of the individuals who had some reason to be angry with Dr. Carnes, at least those who had also been his patients. Reed asked, "Just to set this issue aside,

Miss Brooks, when did you first learn of the death of Dr. Carnes? I presume that you knew about it before we arrived."

"Yes," she said quite curtly, "I knew about his being killed; I heard about it on the radio Sunday morning, and all I can say is that as far as I'm concerned, he got what he deserved. Too bad it didn't happen years ago. If you know what happened to me you should understand how I feel," Marly remarked very clearly, but with an obvious bitterness. She had no trouble giving vent to her feeling; her speech was unimpaired, and stronger than the detectives expected; her hazel eyes flashing with signs of anger.

Detective Reed responded, "We are aware of the problem you had with Dr. Carnes, Miss Brooks, that is why we are here, and we do feel badly about the outcome for you. Unfortunately, we have the task of trying to determine who killed Dr. Carnes and for what reason. We are just at the beginning of our interviews with some of his patients, particularly those who have had some kind of personal problem with the doctor in the past. There is little question that you fall into that category, so we do need to ask you some questions. The first question being, where were you last Saturday evening, between six and seven thirty?"

"That's easy," Miss Brooks laughed, "Here at home, where I always am. Looking like I do, do you think that I would be out on a heavy date? This life is no fun. Who wants to go out with someone that can't hold her head up straight? If I had the money I would even pay a gigolo to take me out," Marly replied, again with bitterness. "Besides that, from what I've heard on the radio, the news people seem to think that it could have just been a robbery by an amateur; do you think that I could have stabbed him and run away with his wallet? For God's sake!"

"We're sorry, Miss Brooks, but we have to ask you these questions. Now for our records, we do have to also ask you whether there is anyone that could vouch for your presence here during the time stated; is there?" Garcia asked, as politely as he could.

"I doubt it," she replied caustically, "but since you are probably going to quiz my neighbors anyway, maybe one of them would have seen through a window that I was at home that night. I can't afford a car anymore; I would have had to have taken a taxi or bus to get to the place where they say that bastard got his due." Marly was clearly distraught, but gathered her wits sufficiently to apologize for her somewhat discourteous behavior. "I'm sorry; I didn't mean to be so rude; I know that you are just doing your job. I hope that you understand that it is difficult for me to forget what has happened to me. This just brings up all of the ugliness again."

Senior Detective Reed responded to Miss Brooks; "No apology is necessary, Marly, we do understand." The two detectives looked at each other, both with the same thought: This isn't going anywhere . . . we're wasting our time. Detective Reed addressed her partner; "Bob, I think that we better move on to following some of the other leads we have. Then she looked at Marly and said, "Thank you for your time Miss Brooks. If we need to talk to you further we will call to set up a time; however, if you should think of something that will assist us in solving this crime, please notify us, if you will." She handed Miss Brooks her card.

"Of course," Brooks quietly replied. "I will be watching the news to see if you have done your job and found the killer; I'd like to know who did it. It's probably someone else that the good doctor screwed up," bitterness still in her voice.

"Oh, we will get the killer, you can bet on that," Garcia replied, "Even though it may take a little while." Then the team left, with Marly Brooks standing by the open door, watching the detectives walk toward their car. Then she closed the door and walked to the kitchen humming a tune, a half smile on her face. She didn't notice that the detectives had veered away from their car, turning instead toward the house to the left of the Brooks' home, where a man holding a well-used yellow handled broom was slowly sweeping the front walkway, in a fashion that made it appear that he was merely killing time, waiting to see who it was that was visiting his neighbor. Both detectives were conscious of the fact that the walk no longer was in need of being swept.

The man with the broom had heard them walking and looked up as they stopped a few feet from him; he halted his needless sweeping and asked, "Can I help you folks?"

"I am Detective Reed and this is my partner, Bob Garcia," Beth announced, as they walked up to the man, simultaneously both showing the man their ID cards. "Would you mind answering a question or two about your neighbor, Miss Brooks?" Reed asked.

"No, not at all," the man replied as he laid down his old broom, "although for the life of me I can't imagine why the police should be investigating her, if that is what you are doing." The man stuck out his hand to Reed and said, "I'm Charles Bingham, and I have lived here since before Marly bought that little house." Garcia also shook the man's hand as Bingham added, "So ask away."

"Please don't jump to any conclusions Mr. Bingham," Reed suggested. "Miss Brooks is just one of several people we have to clear on a recent case; she is merely what we call a person of interest. I don't want to take your time to get into any details right now. We merely want to know if you can confirm whether or not she was at home last Saturday, in the early evening."

"I wish that I could give you a positive answer to that question, but I cannot," Bingham replied. "I really don't socialize with her that much. As I recall, however, I do believe that her house looked dark, but then it always looks dark; she doesn't burn the lights much. My wife, Virginia, who passed away a few years ago, and I knew that she has had only a meager income, but we never knew the source. I suspect that she may actually be on total disability coverage under Social Security. It's a darn sham, a woman that young; she doesn't have much of a life, not since that damn doctor screwed her up."

"You're probably right on that income score," Reed replied, ignoring the comment about the doctor, but then she asked Bingham, who appeared to be talkative:

"How about visitors, friends, relatives, agency representatives, utility workers, other neighbors, or charity helpers? Does she have any visitors at all?"

"Not many," Mr. Bingham replied. "When she first moved in, I think about seven years ago, she had a few young men visit her quite often, presumably dates, and she would go out with them. I believe that she was working at a camera shop in the strip mall at that time, and her Irish accent attracted a lot of young men, but she lost her job when she developed that medical problem. The young visitors stopped coming, almost immediately. Now she hardly goes out of the house; if she goes out for a short walk, which she likes to do every day, it is never in the daytime. About three months ago, there was a man about her age, maybe a little older, who was there for a few hours. I got a pretty good look at him when he arrived because I was doing the same thing I was doing just now, sweeping the walk," the neighbor said, "That's about all I can do, physically, anymore, but it gets me outside. Anyway the young man also stopped by for a few short visits since then. I'm pretty sure that there was one night when they went out for dinner. She's by herself most of the time; I think that she must read a lot, or watch television."

"What about some physical description of her visitor?" Detective Garcia asked. "His size, weight, hair color, clothes?" Garcia asked. "Also, what about his car; did you recognize the make, model, the year, or the color? More importantly, any chance that you remembered anything about his license plate . . . the state and letters or numbers?"

"I didn't see him for very long at any time, and I was never really close to him," the neighbor replied, "From a distance, though, he appeared to be relatively slender, about medium build, maybe five-ten, with dark hair. I caught just a bit of his voice when Marly greeted him at the door, I'm sure that he had a bit of an Irish or Scotch brogue. He could be a relative. I didn't see the kind of embraces that would indicate that they had a personal relationship; no hugs or kisses. I'm sorry not paying much attention about the car; he was parked in the shadows of the house on the other side of Marly's place and I never gave a thought about looking at the license plate; had no reason to, so I can't help you there, sorry."

"Thanks, Mr. Bingham; don't worry about it. We do appreciate the information that you did give us," Detective Reed said while handing him two of her cards. "Please write your phone number on the back of one of my cards; here is a pen." She took the card back from Mr. Bingham after he had written his phone number on it, and then requested him to call her if anything else came to his mind that might seem out of the ordinary in terms of activity next door. Then she added, "We may come back to you later and have you repeat what you have said to us, to a recorder, rather than have you come into headquarters for a deposition. In the meantime, we would like to have you refrain from discussing our visit with anyone, especially Miss Brooks. I don't want you to do anything that you think you shouldn't do, but if you catch the license plate number of that man's car, or its' description, it might prove helpful if you called that in to us. But don't worry about it if you don't catch the plate numbers. We would also not want you to enter into any kind of confrontation with her visitor, because it could make yourself vulnerable to physical harm; he could be dangerous; we just don't know enough about him, so we want to have you play it safe."

"I understand," Mr. Bingham replied; "I'll be careful, and I promise to be discreet, but I will try to pay more attention to his car the next time he visits Marly."

The three shook hands and the detectives left. As they walked to their vehicle, Detective Reed said, "It looks like we have one more character to join the group, but at least he is not another unhappy patient of Dr. Carnes."

"I don't think that he is a very well person, Beth," Detective Garcia stated, "Unless it's a temporary thing; his handshake was like the proverbial wet rag . . . and he's not that old. I can't picture him wielding a knife, or having a motive to commit murder."

"I know," Beth Reed agreed, "but it appears that there's nothing wrong with his mind, and he may eventually be of some real help to us, especially if that visitor of Marly's turns out to be a legitimate suspect for us. I think that we may be looking to him to get more information on the man's car so we can trace it back and find out who he is. As long as he enjoys sweeping his front walk with his old broom," she laughed, "we have a chance of getting more information from him. I hate to call him a busybody because I'm sure that we have both gotten some good information on other cases from the neighborhood gossip or nosy-parker."

Bob Garcia chuckled at his partner's comment and said, "You're right on that score, Beth, and that you agree with me that if we don't hear from him for awhile, we will probably decide to call on him again. If he really isn't well, it could be that he might forget to call us. When we get back into the car, let's discuss our next move. If you agree, I thought that we might question Mrs. Carnes next; you must be as anxious as I am to see what she is like."

"I am, I am," Detective Reed confirmed.

EIGHT

Before Detective Garcia could even start the car after they were buckled in, Beth Reed had her cell phone uncapped and was dialing a number; she looked at her partner and raised a finger to her lips. Garcia uttered a surprise "What? . . ." before he caught the meaning of her gesture and cut short the question he had in mind.

"Cindy, this is Detective Reed," Beth spoke into her phone; "Garcia and I changed our minds and decided that we should follow up quickly on that Carnes divorce situation. So if you have that reporter's calling card handy, would you please give me his name and phone number? I don't know what I was thinking when I had you keep that card."

Cindy still had the card on her desk and was pleased to be able to immediately reply to Reed's request. "No problem, Detective Reed, I have it in my hand right now; do you want his cell phone number as well? It's on the card," she advised.

"Yes, please," Reed responded. She wrote down the numbers, the reporter's name, a Don Fletcher, thanked Cindy for the information and clicked off her phone. Reed then turned to her partner; "I'm sorry, Bob, I should have told you what I was going to do, before I made the call. I know that we told Cindy that we would get the reporter's card later, but I had one of those brain flashes and just had to call right away."

"Hey, no need to apologize, partner," Garcia assured her. "Sometimes those spontaneous thoughts are the ones that solve crimes. So now what? Are you going to just quiz the reporter on the phone, or are we going to try and set up a meeting with him? What's his name?"

"It's Don Fletcher, Bob, and I think that we ought to first see what kind of response and information we can get from him over the phone, and then we can decide what route to take; that should save us some time. The first hope is that he is available by phone right now, and the second one is that he will be receptive to giving us some useful information." Reed laughed when she added, "And I promise you, no more surprises." Garcia joined in the laugh, as his partner punched in the phone numbers for Fletcher given to her by Cindy.

Don Fletcher's cell phone buzzed in his jacket pocket just when he was finishing up his lunch at the Ah Won Chinese Buffet restaurant. He wiped his mouth with a napkin in his left hand while he pulled the phone out of his pocket with his right. He answered the call with a quick no-nonsense response: "Fletcher here."

Detective Reed, sensing the reporter's apparent desire for brevity, wasted few words in introducing herself, describing the objective of her call, and the assignment of the Dr. Carnes case to herself and Detective Bob Garcia. "If this is a bad time to talk a moment about our questions, Don, we could set up a meeting later today or tomorrow, or I could call you at a more convenient time. I know that you reporters are always under some kind of time pressure."

"No, no, detective; as it happens, you couldn't have caught me at a better time," the reporter assured her. "I just finished a delicious lunch of Mandarin Chicken; I'm still right here at my luncheon table, and have plenty of time to talk. I think that we have met before, Beth, on some other case. It is Beth, isn't it? How can I help you?"

"Good memory, Don; Beth is right. Actually we're not sure if you can help us or not, but we're hoping," Reed answered. "We picked up the word at headquarters that you had mentioned to someone there that you knew or had somehow learned that Mrs.

Carnes had filed for divorce just a few days before her husband was murdered. Is that right?"

Fletcher's demeanor improved after he learned who had called him and what the call was about. "From what I know about the case, detective," he said, "you and your partner have a tough nut to crack, and I doubt if I can be of much help to you."

"Well we'll see, Don. As a reporter you know that sometimes it is the most insignificant fact that becomes the most meaningful. Anyway, I don't want to waste your time, but can you give me the date that the divorce papers were filed, the basis of Mrs. Carnes complaint and action, the name of the attorney, anything? We do plan to review the filing papers ourselves, but we want to get something going today, if we can. At the moment we are well away from the court building; hope you understand," Reed continued.

"I do appreciate your situation, detective Reed, and as it happened, what I learned was merely because of a coincidence. I was in the county divorce court building a few days ago, just researching a principal involved in an expose' I am working on, when I bumped into Walter Price. Walter and his wife have been our personal friends for a long time and he happens to be the attorney Mrs. Carnes has hired to handle her divorce. I wasn't previously aware of that fact, but when we met we decided to have a cup of coffee in the snack shop in the building's lower lobby area; it was an opportunity to catch up on each other's personal news. It appears that the connection between Mrs. Carnes and Walter really stems from his wife Sylvia's friendship with the doctor's wife. He told me that the two of them have played tennis with some group at the country club for years. That's how he got her case; he specializes in divorce problems."

"That's very very interesting, Don; we may have to talk to him personally, depending on what develops, or we may even decide that we should interview his wife, since she has been so close to Mrs. Carnes. Anything else?" Reed inquired.

Fletcher was relaxed and seemed to be in no hurry to end the call. "Well this may be of some interest to you, Beth. Price told me that Mrs. Carnes claim of incompatibility appears to be justified, but no physical violence was ever mentioned. He had learned through the wives that the good doctor was definitely addicted to gambling, and spent hours, sometimes days, away at casinos, even out of town. Opal was bored, at least at home, and there did not seem to be much of a sex life anymore. Walt said that that was one of the reasons that she spent so much time at their country club playing tennis and bridge, and at the Garden Club, or doing charity work. She was left to her own devices. Walt's wife had confirmed to him many times that there was never a third party involved; no triangle; Walt had never heard of any extra marital sexual activity by either party. Sylvia was also certain that there were never any serious money problems between them; he never questioned whatever she spent."

Detective Reed interrupted Fletcher, because although it appeared that he had more to say, she felt that he had already given her enough information to have her and Bob work on, and she did not want to impose on him any further. "You have been very helpful, Don, and we appreciate your time and the information you have given us. This is the first time that we have heard of Dr. Carnes' addiction to gambling, which in itself could be a link to someone who might have had a motive strong enough to commit murder. I think that we both understand that everything that you have told us is really hearsay at this point, so unless there is an odd twist in this case, I don't think that you will have to concern yourself about being involved any further in our murder case. We will, without question, obtain legal confirmations on some of that information, from either your friend Price and/or court records. Thanks so much for your input, Don; we owe you one." Fletcher acknowledged the thank you and hung up.

Detective Reed turned to her partner and said, "Apparently Mrs. Carnes hasn't been a very happy wife, and it does appear that she has had a degree of malice towards her husband; she has just been seething with discontentment because the doctor went his own way, the gambling way, while she frittered away her time on the tennis courts and elsewhere. According to what Don's friend told him, Mrs. Carnes' lady friend believes that she just got tired of being married without a husband to share life with; she decided to take the non-violent way to deal with her problem . . . or so it seems on the surface. We have to remember that in a large percentage of divorce cases, the reason given in a divorce filing is often not the basic and true reason for the divorce."

Detective Garcia said, "I know; that's one of the games divorce lawyers play. We might save ourselves some time, Beth, if I made some calls when we get back to the office. I think that once I can get connected to the right parties at each of the major casinos within one or two hundred miles of Orange Grove, we should learn if Dr. Carnes was a high-roller, or not. They may have to call me back at headquarters to confirm my authority to request such information; I expect that. We may also actually learn whether he had a buddy who he gambled with, not just at the casino, but possibly also on a one-on-one basis; that would not be uncommon. Someone like that might have developed into an unhappy adversary, with money being at the center of some controversy."

"You're right there, Bob," his partner confirmed. "I think that that is an excellent idea that might generate some usable information quickly. I've been on the phone a lot today; so it's your turn," she laughed.

NINE

Detective Reed put down the notes and messages that she was reading on top of her desk and looked over at Garcia's work station; she was glad to see that he was not on the phone and decided to walk over to see if he was through making his phone calls. She stopped short of his desk and said, "Well Bob, it looks like you have finished with all of your calls; are you?"

Garcia had seen her approach his area and rose to greet her, not moving from behind his desk. "You guessed right, Beth; I am finished, thank God; my ear is sore. I just got off the horn with a Miss Graham from the Golden Arab. Do you want to sit down here to get the results of my calls, or would you prefer going back to your own office, and to probably a more comfortable chair?"

"No, Bob, this will be fine," she assured him as she eased into his conference chair, and asked, "I hope that were you successful with your calls; how many casinos were you able to contact?"

"I picked the three largest ones I thought were within a reasonable distance from Orange Grove," he responded, "I called the Marquise, the Opulencia, and the Golden Arab. As expected, I had to leave our office number with each one because the first party that I reached did not have the authority to release the kind of information I wanted. As a consequence, I had to play telephone tag all afternoon; it was a drag, but I finally got some good info from each one of them on Dr. Carnes and also on his gambling buddy, who happens to be Justin Douglas, the Carne's lawyer. I was not surprised that Dr. Carnes was well known by some of the people at each of the three casinos. I'm sure that all of the casinos have some kind of system set up with each staff so that they can keep tabs on the high-rollers, which he must have been."

Beth Reed sympathized with Garcia's frustration on the phone, and said, "I'm sorry about your having to make all of those calls, Bob, but you have saved us a lot of time driving around to each of those casinos. Besides, I think that they would rather not have us there in person anyway, even though we're in plain clothes; not good for their image. Do you think that any of the information you got will help us at all?"

"It might, Beth," Garcia answered, "but that will take some thought; we can discuss the results after I finish telling you what I learned, unless you don't think that any further discussion will be necessary. Anyway, let's start with the Marquise. I eventually talked to the manager there and learned that he was well acquainted with the doctor, and knew him to be a regular at the Craps tables as well as being a Blackjack player. Apparently he patronized that casino at various hours of the day or night, and very often he was with another man, who later proved to be Mr. Douglas. However, the manager had no personal information about the companion. He said that as part of their own security system, they daily examine credit card charge slips as a basis for maintaining information on regular players, especially the high rollers. He also stated that the doctor always paid for any drinks or meals that the two of them might have had. He added that the other man with Dr. Carnes always had his own supply of cash for chips or tokens; he never cashed a check at the casino, so they had no record of his name. Just to make sure that the person we were both talking about was really Mr. Douglas, I had him give me the best description of the man that he could. I wrote it down so that we could confirm that fact, but I'm pretty sure that Justin Douglas was the man because of confirmations that I received later at the other casinos," Garcia concluded.

"I guess that report alone clearly confirms the doctor's addiction to gambling," Reed stated, "But it doesn't help us much in determining if Mr. Douglas should be a suspect in the doctor's murder, other than it proves that they had a social relationship. What about the other casinos; were they of any more help?"

"The security chief at the Opulencia is who I talked to there," Garcia replied. "He was also well acquainted with Dr. Carnes; he talked about him almost as though they had been friends. He actually knew Justin Douglas's name; referred to him as Dr. Carnes' "lawyer friend." However, he also voiced some distain for Mr. Douglas, used the term "bottom feeder" in our discussion. I took that to mean that he thought of Douglas as a leech, who took advantage of Dr. Carnes' generosity. As with the Marquise, the chief confirmed the frequency of Carnes visits to the casino, whether he came with Douglas or by himself; he said that Dr. Carnes' visits were at all different hours; sometimes he would play awhile, leave, and then come back later in the same day. I gathered that he was not the kind of player that played for long hours at any one time, at <u>any</u> of the casinos, and no one at the casinos ever said that he had played with any other person, man or woman."

"That all adds up to give Justin Douglas a pretty unfavorable personality; not a very likeable person, but still nothing more, at least at this point. It does, however, bring him up a bit on our list of suspects. As of now, I have him mentally categorized with our character, Zach Segal, but a killer? I don't know. So what about the Golden Arab; any luck there?" Beth Reed asked her partner.

"Not much," Garcia replied. "The assistant manager, the Miss Graham I had just finished talking to when you came over, is also responsible for security at that casino. She said that she has been in that position for fifteen years and remembers when Dr. Carnes was a frequent player there. I asked her what she meant by "was" a player. According to her recall, back when the doctor did play there he was often accompanied by his friend, Mr. Douglas, whom she identified by name. She said that they mostly played the Craps tables, and that they were regulars for several years before an altercation arose that ended their patronage, basically because of Douglas's disruptive conduct."

"Did Miss Graham tell you what happened?" Reed asked.

"Yes, without my even asking; she seemed to be enjoying a break from whatever she does there. Miss Graham said that one late afternoon, Douglas became surly with a cocktail waitress and insulted her in a most ungentlemanly manner; he had been losing at the tables and was not in a good mood. He cursed at her because he thought that she was too slow in bringing him his drink, and that the drink she brought was too weak. The doctor was embarrassed when she called for security, which only made Douglas more unruly and obnoxious. He got into a bit of physical altercation with the security officer. He did get himself roughed up a bit by the guard that tried to settle him down, after Douglas had pushed the guard. In short, he threatened to sue before he was ushered out of the casino. Dr. Carnes, however, did play there a few times after that, alone, but he finally stopped coming to the Golden Arab altogether. Miss Graham offered to let us review the security guard's report of the incident if we wished to do so; I told her that we would consider it, and would contact her later if we felt that it would be necessary. And as with the others, I thanked her for the information and her time." Garcia added, "She then laughingly invited me to return . . . as a player."

"I think that you did a good job, Bob, in getting that much information from the casinos. At this point it doesn't sound as though it would be necessary to see that report from the Golden Arab," Reed said, "but Mr. Douglas does seem to be inviting us to investigate him further. It appears that he does have a streak of violence in his character."

"Do you remember if we included Mr. Douglas in those orders for blood or saliva so we could get his DNA numbers?" Detective Garcia asked Reed. "I don't recall that."

"I thought that we did add him to the list, but I think that it was after our original request was made," Reed replied. "We better check on that as soon as we can. In the meantime, let's give a surprise visit to Douglas' office. I'm curious about his professional operation; just how big it is, what kind of staff he has, or if he is a one-man, one-girl setup. Maybe we will find out whether he owns the furniture and office equipment, of if everything is rented. That would be a sign of something amiss, like he may not be very well off, even if he is a lawyer. We should also check out his residence, the neighborhood, and how long he has lived there. I think that there is a lot more for us to learn about Mr. Justin Douglas."

Garcia asked, "Why don't we check on the Court Order for Douglas now, as long as we are here in the office, and then head to his place of business? That should pretty well kill the rest of the day. It would make it a better end of the day if we could stop at Clancy's for a drink, if you have the time."

"I'd love to, Bob," Reed said, with a tone of obvious regret, "but my brother Craig has invited me out for dinner tonight. He is here on business for just the day, and he has to leave back for Tampa in the morning. I would really like to have him meet you, but I think that it's a little too soon; maybe next time; I think that you would like him. Why don't you check on the Court Order while I dig out Douglas's office address and decide how we should get there."

"That's a good idea; I shouldn't be long, Beth, so I would expect to be back at my station in fifteen or twenty minutes, and then we can take off for LeBland's." He gave his partner a half-wave, and then left for the legal department. He was a little charged up, thinking about this fresh lead to follow. As it turned out, Garcia got his information quickly at the legal department and was back sooner than he expected to be. He went directly to Reed's work station and asked Beth, "Well, are you ready to roll?"

"I thought I would be, Bob," Reed replied, "but I realized I had more time before I had to meet Craig, but I don't think I would have enough time for us to also pay Mr. LeBland a visit. I thought we could see him tomorrow. So if you wouldn't mind my taking the car, I would like to meet the doctor's wife and ask her a few questions. I can cut off my time with her anytime I want to. I hope you don't mind, but my thought was that maybe a woman-to-woman meeting might be more comfortable for her, and then I can drive direct to the restaurant to meet my brother. I called Mrs. Carnes to see if she could meet with me. I got lucky, she is free this afternoon. What do you think? Do you mind?"

"Of course not, Beth, that would be fine with me. My desk is a mess so I could use some time to clean up paperwork and maybe review my notes. Go ahead; you can tell me later what you learned, if anything. Enjoy the dinner with your brother, but I hope we're still on for tomorrow night. I'll make the dinner reservation at Tony's and I'll let you know the time tomorrow; okay?"

"Not this time, Bob; it's my turn. Believe it or not, I can cook. Dinner at my place at six-thirty, cocktails at five-thirty, and who knows what after dinner, unless you're disappointed with the meal," she laughed. "See you tomorrow," she said, still with a coy smile on her lips as she left.

Twenty minutes later Detective Beth Reed was greeted by a pleasant, but unsmiling Mrs. Carnes at her ostentatious home. She held the door open for Reed, and simply said, "Come in."

Reed said "Thank you." as she entered, and then followed Opal to a small sitting room, where she was waved to a sturdy antique chair that carried an elaborate needlepoint seat and back covering. Because Reed did admire the artistry of the chair, and also to help establish a pleasant atmosphere, she said, "What a lovely chair; is it old? I hope you don't mind my asking, Mrs. Carnes."

Mrs. Carnes was surprised to hear a policewoman talking about anything being lovely, but she was still passive when she responded in her unwavering sophisticated manner. "No, I don't mind at all; I appreciate the compliment. As a matter of fact, that chair is quite old," she admitted. "About a hundred and twenty-five years old, to be exact, but it has been restored to almost its original condition, including the needlepoint work. If you are interested in it, Detective Reed, I may be selling it soon, and I would do so at a very fair price. Although it was originally owned by my grandmother, and then by my mother, I have no sentimental attachment to it. I don't even know why I kept it for so long. I never knew my grandmother."

The detective did not expect the woman's reply, but was unfazed and commented further. "It is a beautiful chair, and I love the needlepoint work. If I am able, when the time comes, I would like to take advantage of your offer. But why would you sell it?"

"With Richard gone, this house is just too big for me alone. I am thinking of down-sizing; maybe actually moving out of the area, or taking a series of cruises. I may even consider moving into one of those high-end retirement communities, where they have tennis, golf, a theatre, and so many activities that one would never be bored. The social life, it is said, is often the envy of the younger set. I'm very undecided as to what I shall do, at least at the present time. One way or another, I know that I will be moving."

"I understand, Opal; do you mind if I call you that?" Reed asked.

"No, not a bit; please do," the widow assented. Now I'll try to answer any questions I can, but truthfully, I don't see how I can help you in solving Richard's murder. I have yet to believe it could not have been only some nutty robber who didn't know what he was doing, or some crackpot on drugs. How stupid, however, to just take Richard's wallet and leave his Rolex."

Detective Reed expressed her own feelings on that point, "Yes that would have been pretty dumb if the killer was just a robber, but because of the violent method employed, we have to consider that there may have been a motive other than robbery. Please understand, Opal, that in no way do I wish to disparage your husband's name or reputation, but we are trying to find a link in this case that may lead us to the killer, and that link could be gambling, which we have learned he was addicted to. May I presume that you have been aware of the doctor's addiction to gambling?"

Mrs. Carnes showed no emotion or reaction to that sensitive question, and calmly replied, "Yes, of course, I have been well aware of it; it would have been impossible for me not to have been. Frankly, I didn't care. He always had enough money, and he never questioned me on what I spent. That doesn't mean that I didn't have some qualms on occasion over the years, especially when he would take a long weekend trip to some casino out of town. Of course it was much more of a worry when our children were little. But I don't see how his gambling would have any connection to why he was killed, or who might have done it."

"Did he have a pal, Opal, a gambling buddy; someone he would have visited casinos with, or gambled with, one-on-one?" Reed asked.

Mrs. Carnes replied, "Richard was not an extrovert; how he functioned as a doctor is beyond me; he had to talk to a lot of different people, almost every day, but of course, not on a social level. He was basically a good person, a bit boring, and consequently he had few friends. We socialized very little as a couple. We each had our own lives; we did very little together. We kind of grew apart as the years went by. I don't know if he had any others that went to the casinos with him, but yes, I know that our lawyer, Justin Douglas, often accompanied him on trips to casinos, in and out of the state."

Reed nodded her head, acknowledging that information, and then asked, "To the best of your knowledge, Opal, were there any conflicts between your husband and Mr. Justin Douglas,? From casinos that we have contacted, we have obtained confirmation of the fact that the two of them frequented the casinos together, so we have to consider the possibility of their having some serious conflict at one time or another. Do you know if at any particular time one of them may have owed the other a substantial amount of money?

Mrs. Carnes hesitated for a moment, seemingly unsure of how to respond, almost revealing a reluctance to betray any loyalty to Douglas that she might have had, and not forgetting her dependency on him as her attorney. She finally answered, "Not recently, I'm sure, but some years back Richard loaned Douglas a large sum or money; I never knew how much it was, but I believe that it was all paid back because they continued to have both a business and social relationship. I suppose that there could have been something more recently that I was not aware of; that was a part of Richard's life that I learned years ago not to intrude upon."

"As a matter of routine, Opal," Detective Reed stated, "I also have to ask you if you know anything more about the doctor's murder than you have read or obtained from the police?"

"No, I do not; I wish I did. The whole thing is incredible," Mrs. Carnes replied politely, but quite emphatically.

Detective Reed gave a thought to inquire about the woman filing for divorce, but couldn't find a logical reason to do so. She decided that it was really a personal matter, at least until she and

Garcia found some connection that would dictate otherwise. She rose from her chair and thanked Mrs. Carnes for her time. They walked to the front door together, both pausing at the threshold. "I appreciate your candidness, Opal, and please let me know if you do move. That chair is a beautiful piece of furniture; I would love to have it." She extended her hand to Opal, who took it gracefully for just a second.

Opal Carnes held the door open for the detective and nodded as she acknowledged Reed's comments. "I'll keep your card, detective, and I assure you that I will call you if I move. You have been very polite."

Reed smiled and left Mrs. Carnes looking after her as she descended the front steps, and she wondered whether the widow knew more about the death of her husband than she had said. The widow seemed almost too composed.

As Detective Beth Reed slid into the driver's seat of the car, she began to think about her brother Craig, and also about how her own life had been to this point in time. It was also easy to think about the woman she had just left; a woman who had no incentive to do anything but please herself. A pleasant enough person, but one with no definitive purpose in life other than seeking one self-gratifying moment after another. Beth Reed could not help but compare her own life with that of Mrs. Carnes. Whereas the widow lady had been taken care of quite well during her entire adult life, and probably also as a child, Beth was proud that she had literally worked very hard to achieve her status as a contributing member of society. In a way, Reed almost felt sorry for the woman; her experience with her during the short term of the interview left her feeling that Mrs. Carnes had never really enjoyed the fulfillment of motherhood; she most likely considered it an interruption of her more pleasurable activities. Reed thought, "I'd bet a buck that her children were raised by a nanny. Is she cold blooded enough to commit a serious crime?" Reed wondered. "A murder? Or would she have paid someone to commit the act?"

"What a gap there is," Beth Reed speculated, "between someone like Mrs. Carnes and the family I was born into. Maybe because our family had few assets and little income we all felt that we wanted to improve our status," she thought. "Mrs. Carnes apparently had no incentive to achieve anything in particular in an honest way," Reed thought. Her law enforcement mind made her wonder about how many crimes are the result of the lack of a conscious; people just drifting from a meaningless life into committing a criminal act. Reed continued to muse as she just sat in the car. The meeting with Mrs. Carnes had put her in a pensive mood; she looked at her clock radio and saw that she still had plenty of time to meet her brother. She put her keys in the ignition slot, but then just put her head back on the headrest and closed her eyes.

"Everything has been going wonderfully, up until now," she thought, "but I wish that I had some assurance that it will continue that way," she fretted. "Becoming attached to Bob might be the best thing that's happened to me in quite awhile; he has given me another incentive in life, but how is it all going to turn out? Is one or both of us going to lose our jobs because of our relationship, or be suspended?" Reed continued to question the future. She mentally speculated further: "I think that Bob and I should talk about what could happen; I think that if he believes as I do, that we are not going to be separated; if forced to do so, then we will resign and seek other employment, with separate police departments, even if we have to relocate. Whatever we do though, will have to wait until we solve the murder of Dr. Carnes." She started to think about how long it had been since she last saw her brother and wondered if he had changed much. Before her thoughts went into another direction, her head dropped until her chest; she had fallen asleep, but just for a moment. Someone blowing their car horn nearby awakened her to where she was, and where she should be going.

Reed opened her eyes and glanced at the clock again; "I better get going to meet Craig. He's a pretty smart guy; maybe he will help me decide whether I should stay the course or take another route." she muttered out loud. She turned the key in the ignition and headed to the restaurant.

TEN

Wednesday morning found Zach Segal opening up his antique shop with his keys in one hand while juggling a paper bag with hot coffee in the other. He turned his head around when he heard a noise just as Sam Meyers reached for the door handle to help his friend. "Hey, you startled me buddy; I almost dropped my coffee," Segal exclaimed.

"Sorry, Zach. I tried to call to tell you that I wanted to meet with you this morning, but my cell phone went dead. Anyway, I knew that you'd be here at ten though; you're never late; so here I am. Are you expecting an early customer, or is it okay for us to talk for a few minutes?"

Zach said, "No, no, Sam, I'm not expecting anyone, so we can talk." He invited Sam in and apologized for not having more than just his own cup of coffee, then asked, "You must have something serious in mind, Sam, to catch me just opening up; it must have something to do with what we talked about on the phone; like making money," He laughed. "Let's sit on the stools behind the counter. That okay?"

"Yeah, sure," Sam agreed. "I do have something serious to talk about," he chuckled. "If you agree that money is important. After our discussion the other day, I went right to work to get a plan going that could net us a few thousand. Tell me what you think of this idea: I can get official appraisal forms with complete descriptions and verifications of jewelry described by qualified, certified appraisers, all false of course, but which would pass for the real thing if done properly. Upon your recommendations to Mrs. Carnes, or any other customer of yours that has big money, we can offer beautiful pieces of exquisite jewelry for sale at half of their true value; that is in accord with the appraisals, of course. As an example: The buyer has to cough up a deposit of say $20,000 on jewelry which you would say was available for $40,000 and described in the appraisals at values of $80,000. The balance would be paid later, she would understand. What woman with big bucks wouldn't jump at that? I know that you're a good salesman, Zach, and that you can turn on the charm when you need to. What do you say? How does that grab you?"

"That sounds like half of a plan, Sam, possibly a working plan, but what about the jewelry itself, and how do we come out on top," Zach inquired, with a look of disbelief. "And wouldn't buying jewelry at a fifty percent discount be too suspicious?"

"First of all there will be no jewelry, Zach, it's a scam; don't you see? Wealthy women who have lots of jewelry have a different perspective on buying expensive jewelry; to them it's like buying groceries at a specialty store; they expect to pay a premium, but they still look for bargains." Sammy was very convincing; Zach was skeptical, but still interested.

"That sounds too easy, Sam, but if it works I'd be a happy camper. The antique business has gone to pot since the recession; it's been more of a depression for antique dealers. If I can't generate some other income I may have to close the shop; no point in paying rent for this place if there aren't enough customers coming in the door. I really enjoy this business, and it did make a lot of money for me in the past. Every once in awhile something unusual would be brought in and I would have a chance to make a killing on a painting or a piece of pottery, but not lately. I'm fairly comfortable right now, money wise, but I like the feel of it coming in, and it's not coming in very often nowadays. It's not as much fun as it used to be."

Sammy thought that he had the answer to his friend's lament. "Look Zach, let me explain the whole thing to you again. I can get colored photos of unique pieces of jewelry and have the appraisal forms written up to match the pieces. Your rich bitches can see the pictures and read the appraisal forms to see that they match. Asking for a deposit of say fifteen or twenty thousand on a piece, or pieces, worth over $80,000 and that they can buy for $40,000 will not seem unusual . . . especially if the price asked is half or less than the "actual" value. In a little while after you get the so-called deposit money, you tell the customer that unknown to you, it all involved stolen jewelry, and that you feel terrible. You had trusted the source that you had dealt with before and had had no problems. Your source took the deposit money and you heard that he left for Canada. You explain that you were caught in the middle; you were also a victim, and that you would refund the deposit if you could afford it. You might even bring out a hanky. Hah!"

"That would be pretty tricky, Sam, but if it works I'll get back a chunk of what that bastard Carnes screwed me out of. I have a customer that might buy the story, however, I would sure like to see it worked on Mrs. Carnes. That would give me a lot of personal satisfaction," Zach professed. "I guess if the first sucker resists the offer because the discount might seem too big, we can always reduce it for the next pigeon. But what about the police? Wouldn't the woman go to the cops right off the bat when she found out that she had been swindled? I like the idea of making some dough, Sammy, but I'm not in great physical shape and I'm too old to spend the rest of my days in prison, sleeping on a cot, with no booze, and staring out a barred window. No amount of money would be worth that."

"Not to worry," Sammy consoled his co-conspirator. "I know that you could sell a refrigerator to an Eskimo, Zach, and I think that you could pull it off, particularly if you try your customer first rather than Mrs. Carnes; we might even let her be number two. I know that you would really like to use her, but she may know your name from the doctor, and may even know the details of the deal that he had with you. Besides that, you apparently have already established a good relationship with the woman customer you mentioned; that should give you some credibility with her." Zach showed his lack of enthusiasm in what Sammy had said, but he recognized the probability that it could work. "Look Zach, if our victim realizes that she may have been involved in a crime," Sam continued, "She is unlikely to go to the police. At the status level that she enjoys I would be surprised as hell if she were to tell anyone of her involvement with stolen property; she would be ashamed to tell anyone, maybe not even her husband, if she is married. Fifteen or twenty grand probably wouldn't make a dent in her net worth. She has to be in a high bracket if she is thinking of spending a chunk on jewelry for her daughters' anniversaries, as you said. I think that the worst thing that could happen is that you would lose a customer from your shop."

"Okay, Sammy, you've never let me down before, so let's go for it," Zach finally agreed. "I know that you don't have enough green to pay off your forger and for the photos we need; I can handle that, just let me know how much you need." Zach offered. "I think that I'll call my customer and warm her up by asking about what kind of pieces she likes or would be interested in; that way we can customize the photos and appraisals to match what we think she might buy into. That would make the whole thing more credible. You want to use good color photos, bright, and large enough to really hold someone's attention."

"That's a great idea, Zach. In the meantime I'll try to get an idea as to how much money I'll need; I'll get back to you on that as soon as I can, maybe even by this afternoon."

"You've got me feeling good, Sam. We've been talking so long that it's almost lunch time. Why don't I close up the shop now, and I'll pop for lunch and a beer. It might give us a chance to run through the plan once more, maybe improve on it."

"Hey! Hey!" Sammy joyfully exclaimed. "I'm all for that. How about Jule's Place? He's got the sexiest waitresses."

"Let's go," Zach said as he pulled out his car keys, "I'll drive. Your idea, Sam, is shaping up to possibly be a lot of fun for us."

ELEVEN

Detectives Reed and Garcia had previously agreed to meet for coffee at Mimi's café early Wednesday morning to plan their investigations for the day, and for the rest of the week; both were a bit unhappy with the progress of their investigation of the murder to this point. They were each rifling through their notes, piecing together what they had learned, but neither of them could come up with anything that they could get excited about as a clue to which individual named by Anne showed the most promise as a suspect. Without having anything actually definitive, they also realized that the killer might not be any one of them, but someone who has not yet been identified. Finally Detective Reed raised her head from her notes, shook short black hair, and in a frustrated, but determined manner gave her suggestion.

"Why don't we check out Mr. LeBland first, Bob?" Detective Reed asked her partner. "If he is still at the office address shown on his calling card, it would be convenient for us; his office is very close to where we are right now."

"Do you realize, Beth, that we are now also not very far from the crime scene?" Bob Garcia asked in return. "I'm thinking that if LeBland is not available to meet with us when we get there, and I agree that we should hit there first, we can go on to the convenience store. By the time we get there it will probably be too early for that night clerk to be on duty, but at least we can find out when he will be. The report by the officers originally called to the scene may also have the man's home address and phone number, so if he isn't on duty we can call him or talk to him at his home. He may be so freaked out by the murder that he may have asked for some time off; I'm really anxious to talk to him. What do you think?" Garcia asked.

"Well slug down your coffee, partner, and let's hit the road. If we can interrogate both possible suspects this morning we should be able to zero in on somebody, either that or we'll have to take a completely new direction." Reed said, with a bit more enthusiasm than she had been showing. "I think that we both feel as though we're stuck in a mud hole; I need some action to perk me up; maybe today's the day."

Garcia was glad to see his partner generate some spark, he liked to see her blue eyes sparkle because that meant that she was likely to come up with some fresh ideas. They had worked together for only three months, and even though she was his superior, she had made him feel like an equal, which he appreciated. He gulped down the remains of his coffee and rose to go, saying, "I'll get the tab and tip if you'll pull out the address of LeBland's office and then help me find the place. I don't know this side of town very well; otherwise I might drive around in circles." Reed laughed at that while she pulled up the address on her GPS. She knew the route even before they got to the car.

"His office is at 1224 East Lake Avenue, which is only a mile east of Central," Beth Reed said, "And it should be on the north side of the street. The card indicates that it is in suite B-202, which is probably on the second floor. I've been in that building before; the rent there is not cheap. They even have potted plants in their parking lot."

They reached LeBland's suite and Reed's assumptions were correct as to its location in the building. The office door was unlocked when they entered, and the detectives were impressed with the furnishings and the size of the facility. However, they were also disappointed to hear from the receptionist that Mr. LeBland was out of the office, and would not return until Thursday morning. Beth Reed introduced herself and Bob Garcia; they each showed the young lady their identification, and left a calling card with the request that LeBland call one of them in the morning to arrange an appointment as soon as possible. No explanation was given as to why they wished to meet with the man, other than it was in connection with a crime. The receptionist was a little disturbed when she learned of their identity and the purpose of their visit, but she agreed to inform her boss as soon as he returned to the office, or sooner if he called in. The team left without any further discussion.

Back in their car, Reed said, "Well, Bob, I guess we better head over to the convenience store, but this early in theafternoon we may be out of luck with the clerk. I suspect that he won't be starting his shift for another hour or two, unless they have changed his schedule. Who knows? Maybe we'll get lucky."

"Might as well," Garcia agreed as he started up the car again. They arrived at the store in less than half an hour, parked, and noted that there were no other vehicles in the parking area provided in the front of the store. Detective Garcia said, "It looks like the murder has kept customers away from the store. Maybe they closed after last Saturday night; well if they did, they must have reopened because it looks like most of the lights are on. It must be open," he said as they exited their vehicle.

As the detectives entered the market, the male clerk looked up with apprehension in his eyes, but became relaxed as the detectives flashed their badges even before they spoke. Detective Reed introduced herself and said, "This is my partner, Detective Garcia. We are investigating the killing of Dr. Carnes that took place here last Saturday, in the early evening. We were given the name of Peter Sandvick as the clerk who was on duty at the time. We know that his schedule is for the evenings, but we were in the vicinity and thought we might learn something by stopping by anyway."

The clerk showed a little nervous emotion, but replied, "Well I am Peter Sandvick, and I was on duty here that night. After last

Saturday's excitement, I asked to be put on an earlier shift; I thought that I would be a little uneasy on the night shift, at least for awhile. Actually, I don't think that I will ever go back on a late shift; I'd probably always be worried. A beer run is one thing, murder is something else."

"Good thing we decided to stop in now, Peter, and found you on duty; it saves us another trip," Reed said. "We do have the information that you gave the officers last Saturday, but we were hoping that in the meantime something else may have come to your mind about the man that you saw briefly near the victim. He may not be the killer, but he could have seen what was about to happen, or saw it happen, and got scared and got out of there quickly. He may also have been the reason the killer didn't have time to take the victims' watch, that is if he intended to take it. One way or another, he is without question a person of interest, and we would really like to talk to him. So far, publicizing the search for him on TV hasn't generated any responses. I apologize for having to ask you to repeat what you told the original investigating officers, but we want you to do so, just in case you may have forgotten something the first time."

The clerk looked a little helpless, as though he wished that he knew more about the mysterious individual; he acted very unsure of himself. "I . . . I thought that I told the other officers all that I knew about the man; I only saw him for a brief moment through the window before I had to answer the phone. I told those officers I thought the man was average height, almost the same as Dr. Carnes, fairly slender. I did not see his hair color because it was quite dark and he was wearing a hat."

Both detectives looked at each other in surprise, and Beth Reed said, "A hat?" I don't recall reading anything about a hat in the officers' report; do you Bob?"

"No, I don't," Garcia responded. "Maybe we missed it, but I hardly think so." He asked Sandvick, "Are you sure that you reported to the officers that Saturday night that the man was wearing a hat?"

"I . . . I think I did, but I was a little shook up, and maybe I didn't. Dr. Carnes stopped in here quite often; before Saturday night I never knew his name, but I knew his face. He was a good customer. It shook me up. Right in front of the store!"

"Okay, okay; that just proves why we have follow-up calls, Peter. But let's not sweat over that right now. Tell us, though, what about the hat? Was it a dress hat, a baseball cap, or a hunter's cap, or what?" Detective Reed probed, a bit irritated that the man had not recalled the cap before now.

The mild mannered clerk squirmed, showing his guilty feeling for possibly not reporting seeing a hat or cap. "I . . . I really didn't think too much about it at the time. A hat's a hat. It was so small; maybe that's why I didn't think too much about it. I could be wrong, but from the glance that I had of it before the phone rang, in the dark and through the window, I think that it could have been a beret or tam, as they call a hat like that, or maybe even a skull cap, a yarmulke; we have quite a few Jewish people in this area," the clerk said, almost showing again some embarrassment for possibly not giving that information originally. Like an afterthought, he added, "It was way too dark to tell what color it was. When I got off the phone, which was only seconds later, I looked out and he was gone; his car was the only one in the lot."

"We understand, Peter." Reed assured him, calming down a bit herself; she put the man at ease, saying, "Don't feel badly, Peter, things like that happen all the time; that's why we have repeat calls. We often learn the most important things and get better clues later, after witnesses and others have settled down and have had an opportunity to re-think events that have occurred. We may get back to you again, but for now just relax. I don't believe that you are in any kind of danger. Whether it was a random robbery that resulted in the murder, or even if it was a premeditated act, whoever did it would have no interest in you. They would surely know that there is no way that you could identify them. Be advised, however, that at some later date you could be called upon to confirm in court what you have told us now, so please inform us if you change jobs or move your residence. We appreciate the information you've given us Peter, but if something else comes to your mind from that night, please give us a call."

The detectives left the store, and as they walked to their car, Garcia said, "Well, Beth, it seems like we have to find out more about the mystery man. If he was not the killer, maybe he could tell us a little more about the last minute or so before Carnes was murdered. Then too, he may want to avoid any contact with the police, either because he may have a record, be on parole or probation, or he could be one of those people who just doesn't want to be involved. It burns the hell out of me to think that some people don't realize how important it is to help the police, especially if they have actually been a witness to a crime. Anyway, at least now we know about the hat, cap, or whatever. The little bit of description that he did give us seems to dictate that at least it was not a golf cap; if it had been a cap with a golf-type visor on it, I think he would have noticed that, even in poor light."

Reed concurred, "Yes, Bob, and it is one more piece of the puzzle . . . maybe an important one. What worries me is that if Sandvick didn't originally recall seeing the hat; what else might he have forgotten to mention? I think that we might have to pay our clerk another visit, soon. Right now we have to call the office and have them get in touch with Hobson. If I remember right, I think that he was going to be out of the office again on another homicide case. I don't know how he can keep track of twelve detectives and lord knows how many cases. It's a wonder that he doesn't have an ulcer. Anyway, he may be miffed if we didn't let him know right away about the cap, even though it may just wind up as a dead end. He may call in the original investigators to see if they just forgot about the hat in the write-up of their discussion with Sandvick, or possibly the typist goofed. Anyway, I'll call the office while you drive."

As they started driving, Detective Garcia commented on the clerk that they had just questioned. "Well that revelation may prove to be one of the best clues we have had so far, and Sandvick may not be the sharpest knife in the drawer, but you have to feel sorry for him; he's almost a nervous wreck."

"Well I never heard that expression before, but it makes the point," Reed responded.

TWELVE

As they had agreed upon Tuesday afternoon over the phone, Nurse Anne Whitcomb and attorney Justin Douglas met at the clinic Wednesday morning. Douglas arrived at exactly nine o'clock and found Whitcomb already there with the front door propped open. She was wearing jeans, a white shirt with rolled up sleeves, and sandals; her graying dark brown hair was pulled back into a bun and tied with a small silver clip. It was obvious to the attorney that she was prepared for a field day, to clean out files, trash what was not necessary to be kept for tax or legal purposes, and to probably vacate the premises. Anne, having met Mr. Douglas during some of his past visits to the clinic to have Dr. Carnes sign forms of one kind or another, expected him to arrive in his usual blue suit, blue shirt, and expensive kaleidoscope tie, which was exactly the way he was attired when he arrived. No one could ever accuse him of being underdressed for any occasion. His dress was a reflection of his personality; he dressed to impress. He was a good looking fifty-eight year-old man, which belied his personality. He entered the office with a directness that did not surprise the nurse; she was accustomed to his being in a hurry, with a direct attitude that required those that he addressed to respond quickly, or incur his displeasure.

On his first visit to the clinic after Anne had started work there, she had naively mistakenly interpreted his manner as being very business-like, but soon realized that he was simply a brash, commanding, controlling type . . . and she really was not looking forward to doing any work with him. However, she realized that she had no choice; she was not in a position to object to his brusqueness. She was determined to not let his personality upset her any more than she had already experienced with the doctor's death, and greeted him as politely as she would have any other visitor to the clinic.

She rose from her chair as she saw him enter. "Good to see you again Mr. Douglas. I never dreamed that we would ever have to meet under these circumstances. I presume that you were as shocked as I was as to what happened to Dr. Carnes," she asked in a questioning way, but she received no immediate response to the implied question.

"Yes, yes," the lawyer replied quickly, appearing as though he did not want to enter into a discussion of the murder, but wanted to get into the questions he had in mind. After some hesitation, however, he decided to make some comment. "Yes, it is a horror that is difficult to comprehend. We can only hope that it was a rare random action, not a murder that was premeditated. From what I have read about the crime, since the killer did get the doctor's wallet, it would appear to have been a robbery gone bad. From my point of view, it doesn't make sense for someone to be killed just for a man's wallet. I've read that the killer, for some reason or another, did not take Dr. Carnes' Rolex watch. Well there's nothing much we can do about it, so let's get on with what needs to be done here. I'm pretty busy with other legal work so I'd like to get this done as quickly as possible." It was obvious that he did not want to spend any time sympathizing with Nurse Whitcomb, or even inquire as to how this tragedy was going to affect her life. Anne was hesitant to ask him any questions, but she had to know just how she was to be employed and how she was to be compensated for her time. She considered deciding to wait for a little while, thinking that Mr. Douglas would settle down a bit, which might make it easier for her to ask him some questions about her own situation. She decided to put her timidity aside and get some answers to the questions that were bothering her.

"Of course Mr. Douglas," Anne acknowledged, "Just tell me what you need or what you want me to do. I'm just as anxious as you are to get this closed up, and I hate to appear self-centered about the work to be done, but since this job is my only source of income, I would also like to know if I will be compensated for my time before we go any further with what has to be done." Anne asked as politely as she could, trying to hide her apprehension as to how he would answer.

Showing a bit of irritation, Douglas responded, "Of course you will be paid," he said gruffly; "But at this point I cannot say how long it will be necessary for you to assist me in closing up the business, and I certainly cannot guarantee your continued employment here if the clinic is sold to another dermatologist. I have an executed power of attorney from both Dr. Carnes and from Mrs. Carnes, so I can pretty much do what I wish. There is ample money in the business account, I am sure, and there must be some accounts receivable that we will pursue for collection. You will be paid for your time on the same basis as you have been in the past," he said as he showed further agitation. "Now let's get on with the work."

Anne was satisfied with Douglas's response and asked, "Well what information do you want first?" She had thought of offering the man some fresh coffee, but with his attitude she thought better of it. She thought that she might be tempted to spill it on him.

Attorney Douglas handed Anne a typed piece of paper as he said, "Here is a list of items that I require, but you may know of things that I am not informed about, so I would appreciate your adding any items that may connect with the items on my list. As you can see, the top items are marked as being of a critical nature. The accounts receivable, the status of accounts that have been turned over to a collection agency, the individual unpaid bills, the bank statements for the last three months, the checks that are outstanding, the business check book, Dr. Carnes' personal check book if it is here rather than at his home, and anything else that is of a financial nature. I may have a copy of his lease agreement for this space in my office, but if you find one here, all the better. I'll need the names of any clubs or organizations that the doctor belonged to, and any charitable groups that he supported. All of those people must be notified. For those items at the bottom of the list, you can take your time; they are of only minor concern."

Nurse Anne scanned the list and then asked, "What about the police? They have been here twice already. Because of the crime involved, shouldn't they know that you are the attorney involved, and that I am working with you to close up or sell the practice? And am I supposed to keep Mrs. Carnes informed about what you, or I am doing? Mrs. Carnes and I have already talked a little, but mostly about the crime; we didn't get into anything about the business of the clinic. I know that she had very little to do with the doctor's business, but wouldn't she want to know what's happening here?"

"No, no, there is no need for you to bother Mrs. Carnes," Douglas sharply replied to Anne. "I will be meeting with her over several matters shortly, and we will be reviewing the progress we make here. Unless she calls you, I would not bother her. I will have my secretary call the police and inform them as to my position, but let me know if there are any problems with the investigators. You said that they have been here twice. Tell me what has transpired with them, and write down their names and phone numbers for me," he ordered.

Nurse Anne was uncomfortable with Douglas and the way he was directing her activities; she felt that he was trying to control her every move, but she had to go along with his directions. She wanted to be paid for her time, yet she also wanted to be doing the right thing for Mrs. Carnes, and for the police. Nevertheless, she detailed the discussions that she had had with the detectives, and handed him the names and phone numbers of the detectives that she had written down. Douglas seemed satisfied and didn't push for any further information. He gave her his card, saying, "Note that the address on the card is probably different than that which you have in your files. I moved my office into a better location a few months ago; however, the phone number is the same. I have already been in touch with Dr. Carnes' accounting firm and I will be working with them after I receive the records that you will provide. I think that you already know Mr. Hurley, the CPA, and if he calls you, just refer him to me. After you provide me with the information that I have requested, Hurley will be working with me or my assistant, so he shouldn't need to bother you." Without thanking Nurse Whitcomb for her time and cooperation, Douglas merely picked up his briefcase and nodded to her, "I'll check back with you in a day or two, unless you find some need to call me sooner." With that he left abruptly, leaving Anne Whitcomb in sort of a tizzy.

"That man doesn't give a damn about Dr. Carnes being killed," she said to herself. "I'll bet that his only concern is how much money he can get out of settling the doctor's affairs. Opal doesn't have a hint about how her lawyer is probably going to screw her out of some of the money in the clinic's accounts, or from the sale of some of the assets. The SOB! Maybe he's even glad the doctor's dead . . . or maybe. Well, I wouldn't be surprised if . . . oh the hell with it," she said disgustedly. "Who cares what I think?" She then turned back to the list that Douglas had given her, without any enthusiasm for what she had to start doing.

THIRTEEN

Detectives Beth Reed and Bob Garcia met again with Chief Detective Clyde Hobson on the Thursday morning following the meeting with the convenience store clerk, Peter Sandvick, and reported the conversation that they had had with the clerk. Hobson sat back in his executive chair and frowned, combing his thick brown mustache with his fingers. "That worries me," he said. Do you think that he knows more than he told you? I find it hard to believe that he did not mention a hat or cap to the original investigating team, or for that matter, why the team didn't probe further to find out about the cap. I intend to have a talk with the senior officer on that original investigation. I don't think that you're through with Mr. Sandvick, but before you hit him again I want you to pursue the LeBland guy. We don't know much at all about him, and from what the Whitcomb woman said, it seems that he would be as likely to have it in for Carnes as much as the other two suspects. Incidentally, the forensics people have finished with Carnes' body and with the murder scene."

Beth Reed interrupted Hobson and asked, "Did they come up with anything that will help us? We still don't have enough material facts that would take us strongly toward any particular person; we're lacking leads."

"I know, I know, Beth. I was coming to that, but I was glad you broke in; it gave me a second to take a slug of my coffee. Now the opinions given me by forensics were that there was definitely only one stab wound, and that Carnes died immediately because it went right to his heart. They told me the way the knife went in, and the way it was twisted, created an unusual amount of blood; apparently it just spurted out like a water fountain. There were no other marks of trauma to the body, so he wasn't beaten up beforehand. He probably died before he even knew what was happening to him." Hobson continued the report, pausing to evaluate the reception of what he had said, while sipping more coffee.

"The knife that was used is believed to have been slender and about eight inches, not a Bowie or hunting knife, but likely a good strong kitchen or utility knife, which we will likely never find. The wound to the heart indicated that the killer violently twisted the knife as it entered the body, to double ensure that Carnes would die quickly, and/or because he was taking out some anger on the doctor. The manner in which the crime was committed leaves no doubt in my mind, and probably in yours, that this was not just a robbery gone bad, but that Carnes was pinpointed and that the murder was premeditated. Everyone involved in either examining the scene or the body has agreed the murderer has to have had blood somewhere on his clothes and maybe part of his own body. Because of the haste with which the crime was committed, it is also possible that the killer might have cut himself slightly; the point being that there may be a drop of blood someplace that came from the culprit. I think that we have to believe that we are looking for a cold blooded killer. As I said, we have to go back to that store clerk and quiz him some more on that so-called witness. But before you do, I have a gut feeling that we must first get a handle on LeBland. So find out when he will be back and get an appointment; it sounds as though he is a busy man, or he is dodging us. If you can't see him very soon, then go ahead and interrogate Sandvick again. In either situation, call me if anything new pops up. This case seems to have a lot of angles and it has all of the potential to eventually surprise us." He leaned back in his chair as if he were finished, but continued on. "Oh, and stop by your desks on the way out and pick up some notes I had forensics write up for you, which includes a confirmation of Dr. Carnes' blood type and his DNA. I can see the possibility that somewhere down the line we may be required to issue search warrants to allow us to examine all of the clothing in someone's closet. As a matter of fact, I don't think that we can delay on that; if we don't check out the clothing quickly the blood evidence will have disappeared. I believe that blood, rather than anything else, will be the connecting link to whoever murdered Carnes. I will be out of the office until Monday, but if you come up with anything hot, the office can get in touch with me, if you call in." The team rose from their conference chairs to leave as Hobson waved them off.

As they were walking to their car, Detective Garcia said to his partner, "Would you mind, Beth, if we stopped for an early lunch? I was up longer than usual last night; got involved in an old movie, and I slept in a little this morning; didn't even have time for coffee, or even juice. Besides that, after hearing those gory details I need to get those visions of all of that blood out of my mind." Actually, that was merely an excuse; Garcia had another thought in mind besides breakfast.

Reed perked up and replied, "You must have been reading my mind, Bob, so help me; I was about to ask you the same thing. I dropped my coffee pot, made a mess in my kitchen, and then I had to change my blouse. Let's go to JB's again, if you don't mind; they make great omelets." She put aside her detective's face and gave Garcia a pleasant smile, which he returned.

They settled in a booth at JB's, one on each side of the table that was meant for just two, and asked the waitress for coffee when she brought them menus. Then they quietly scanned the luncheon menus to make their selection. Garcia said, "Well I guess we're too late for breakfast, so I'll have my favorite sandwich, a Rueben."

"That's too heavy for me," Beth responded, "I eat a lot of tuna fish, helps to keep my weight down. Since I can't have one of their omelets, I'll have to settle for my favorite, a tuna salad sandwich with fruit on the side."

The waitress brought them their coffee and asked if they were ready to order. They each gave her their respective selections. As they simultaneously took their first sips of coffee they silently stared at each other; it seemed accidental, but it wasn't. Garcia broke the "spell" by asking, "You know, Beth, we have worked together for over three months and I think that all we know about each other is that we are both single. That's right, isn't it?"

"Divorced single, yes, since almost two years ago. Long story, probably boring, at least it was for me. It was such a drag that I almost feel as though I was never married." Beth Reed continued, "Easy to forget, and better than remembering. There, that breaks the ice, now how about you? Any dark secrets?"

"Nothing profound, but I was engaged once, for a few months," Garcia said, "Nice girl; it could have worked out, but religion got in the way. She was into it too deeply, which took me awhile to realize. I have been slowly going in the opposite direction. We parted as friends; we both realized that the issue was too serious for her to overcome, especially because her whole family was of the same conviction. I see her once in awhile; no spark left. I haven't clicked with anyone since, and that's over a year ago, not that I haven't had my eyes open. Maybe I'm too particular. I've read that as you get older you tend to find it more difficult to match up. I know that there are a lot of positive things about being married though, so I haven't given up. I also agree with what the experts say, and that is that each of us, consciously or unconsciously, wants to have somebody to spend our later life with; they say it makes that time happier and life a little longer. There, now you have my philosophy of life," he laughed, but at the same time viewed his partner with a concern as to how she reacted to what he had said.

The waitress brought their orders and more coffee, and as Garcia shifted his body to sit up better to eat, his left foot unintentionally touched Reed's. She didn't move, and he felt a slight tinge of excitement throughout his body, but he settled down to eat, not allowing himself to think that the touch meant anything. Instinctively, at that moment he looked up and saw his partner staring at him. Up to that time, he had never seen her smile just like that; it was a quiet, happy smile, and he was encouraged to ask, "I don't want you to think that I am getting too personal, Beth, but may I ask if you are seeing anyone, or are you turned off men now?"

"It's okay, Bob," Reed answered. "That's a normal question, and no, I am neither turned off men nor am I seeing anyone at this time. Frankly being a policewoman is a turn-off for a lot of men; they see someone in that position as being pushy or controlling, too masculine, or even anti-sexual. After one bad experience, it becomes more difficult to find someone who fits the image of what one expects, just as you have said. I actually try to put my police personality aside in my private life, and suppress any aggressive traits. During the time that I have been on the force I have had plenty of advances from my fellow officers, most of whom were married . . . they were just looking for something extra. They were a little disappointed." Garcia smiled at his partner across the table, seeing her in a new light. He reached over and just lightly touched her left hand, and asked, "If you are not interested, it's okay Beth, but do you think that we might have dinner out some evening? I'm not involved with anyone and it would give us both an opportunity to see what we are each like when we're not doing police work." He looked into Beth's clear blue eyes, which had a gem-like sparkle to them, and waited for a reply.

"I would love to have a dinner out with you, Bob," Reed responded, "whether it will go any further or not, but we do have a problem. As partners, traveling in the same car, spending hours together investigating crimes, having, you might say, a lot of exposure to each other, might be against department policy, not to mention the problems we could have while riding in a police car, if we did get involved. I can envision a lot of will power and restraint would be called for; after all, police detectives or not, we are human. I like you, Bob; we have gotten along very well in the months we have worked together, and I would really like to keep you as a partner. At least we know that we are compatible as partners on the force. Why don't we do the dinner thing, see what happens, and then we can decide where we'll go from there?"

"You're so damn smart, Beth; you should make chief detective someday. You laid it out perfectly, and I agree one hundred percent. Maybe it will all fall apart when we have dinner, and if it does, I would hope that we would still be friends, and partners. How about if I call you after I make a reservation for this Saturday night?"

Detective Beth Reed reached her hand out and squeezed Garcia's, saying laughingly, "Well partner, I'll be waiting for your call. Now the next thing we have to learn is each other's Zodiac sign." Garcia joined in the laugh.

FOURTEEN

Before lunch was finished, the detective team agreed to check by Roland LeBland's office, to either interrogate him if he was available, or to make an appointment to do so later. Hobson hadn't said anything about pursuing Zach Segal, but since his antique shop was also on the same side of town as LeBland, the detectives planned to stop there as well. The convenience store would be the last call, unless they got hung up before that. They put aside the personal thoughts that they had at lunch and drove rather silently to their first stop.

When they arrived at LeBland's office, the receptionist rose to meet them, looking surprised at their appearance. She stated, "I informed Mr. LeBland about your first visit and your plan to return. I think that he has been expecting you to call for an appointment, however, I think that he's free at the moment so he might be able to see you right away. Let me check." She called him on the intercom phone, and informed LeBland as to who was here that wished to see him. She then announced to the detectives that he had told her to usher them in to his office, which she promptly did, and then left.

LeBland rose and extended his hand to Reed as she introduced herself, "I am Detective Beth Reed and this is my partner, Bob Garcia. We apologize for not calling to see if you were available to meet. We changed our plans for the day sort of at the last minute." The two men just nodded to each other as they shook hands. "Thank you for making yourself available Mr. LeBland,"

"Well I guess you were lucky that my schedule was clear for this time, so no apology is necessary. I have an hour that's free, so how can I help you?" LeBland asked, in a very business-like manner.

Detective Reed responded. "We are investigating the murder of Dr. Richard Carnes, whom we understand treated you in the past. We have assumed that you have read about his murder."

LeBland showed no surprise or any other emotion, but waved them towards two conference chairs as he returned to his own chair. "Oh, yes, I did read about it. I can't say that I feel very badly about it; I'm not celebrating it, but I sure as hell don't feel badly about it. I'm sure that you know about the rotten deal I had with him; no doubt that's why you're here." With an obvious bitterness, he voiced his anger toward Dr. Carnes, and became a bit agitated as he spoke. "Frankly, I hope the son-of-a-bitch rests in hell! When you find out who did it, let me know, I want to thank the party." LeBland was a big man, a bit beefy, with a redness in his face that indicated possible high blood pressure, or a reflection of having enjoyed too many cocktail parties. Nurse Whitcomb's notes stated that he would now be about fifty-five; he looked a decade older.

Detective Garcia asked, "Just exactly what happened, Mr. LeBland, that caused the friction between you and the doctor? We have received no detailed information on that issue; so we have only a general idea."

"It was a straight forward deal, I thought," LeBland responded, "and because I was dealing with a doctor, my dermatologist; I mistakenly believed that I could trust the man. I was wrong. We had met at a casino by coincidence sometime after he cleared up my rash, and then we had lunch a couple of times and discussed investments. We had agreed to purchase a commercial building together, with the thought that we would both move our offices into it and rent out the balance to other tenants. We agreed on the price, and to save his time I put up all of the earnest money, which was $50,000. That sounds like a lot for just earnest money, but not on a million dollar building. Anyway, to get the price that we were happy with, we agreed to have the contract read that the earnest money was not refundable if we backed down. It never entered my mind that we would ever cancel the agreement. Well our good doctor changed his mind, and I lost $50,000 because I could not financially handle buying the building by myself. He should have come up with the $25,000, which was his half. Yeah, I was pissed off, and still am, but not to the point where I would have killed the bastard." As he finished he was breathing heavily and was even more flushed. He reached for a tissue from the box on his desk and wiped the perspiration from his forehead; he then reached into his desk drawer, came up with a little reddish pill, which he swallowed without any water.

The detectives looked at each and it was apparent that they could not believe that this man, himself, could have killed Dr. Carnes. If he were involved, it would have to have been that he paid someone else to do the job. Both detectives assumed that the pill he had taken was for high blood pressure. Reed asked, "Mr. LeBland, we understand how you feel, but we have to pursue every lead possible in order to solve this crime, so I do have to ask, where were you last Saturday evening?"

LeBland looked as though he was surprised at being asked that question, but he gave a little shrug to his shoulders and replied, "Christ! That's an easy question to answer; I was in Miami with my wife for a long weekend and to meet some other commercial real estate brokers. We stayed at the Long Beach Hotel, should you wish to check."

"Thank you," Reed said, "Just one more question that I am obligated to ask. Did you have anything to do with the murder of Dr. Carnes, directly or indirectly?"

LeBland did not hesitate to respond, stating forcefully, "Hell no, I did not! Not that I never thought that someone should knock off the jerk. I'm probably not the only person that hot-shot doctor screwed."

The two detectives again thanked LeBland for his time, shook his hand, and left after advising him that it might be necessary for them to meet with him again, or that he could be called into court to confirm his statements. He merely nodded in assent, but the look on his face indicated that he knew that the detectives would likely return.

When the detective team settled back in their car they sat quietly for a moment to reflect on Mr. LeBland. Garcia broke the silence, asking his partner, "What do you think, Beth, is that guy a potential suspect?" He sure as hell still has enough anger towards the victim to have wanted the man dead."

Reed answered, "There is no doubt about that, Bob, and I agree that if he is involved, he doesn't strike me as being the someone who would have wielded the knife. We can't let him off the hook yet, though. We have to check out the Miami trip time first, and then determine if he has had any associations with individuals who would have been capable of doing a killing. It wouldn't hurt to give the state Board of Realtors a call and see if he has a clean slate with them. We might also give some thought to getting a list of his lower level employees and check them out as to whether any of them have a felony record. Regardless of his loss, it's obvious that he still has the kind of money that it would take to hire a killer, or at least he puts on that kind of front. For the moment, let's put that aside and go see if our antique dealer is open. We haven't given him any attention so far, and his place is almost just around the corner."

"That's fine by me, Beth," Garcia agreed. "Of the three names given to us by Miss Brooks, we know the least about the cause of Segal's anger toward Dr. Carnes.

Nurse Whitcomb just said that there was some kind of a financial deal that went sour, and that he blamed the doctor. Personally, I find that it is hard to believe that some guy in the antique business would be involved in a killing. People that run that kind of business are more apt to be the gentler kind, arty types."

"You're right about that, Bob, but then how often do we have a mild mannered school teacher or bookkeeper, male or female, guilty of murdering an unfaithful lover or a boss that they have come to hate. Profiling has been of some help in police work, but we have all been fooled by it at one time or another. They come in all shapes and sizes."

"No argument there, Beth. Guess I need more experience in profiling, it can be misleading." Garcia acknowledged. "On to Auld Lang Syne."

As Garcia turned on the ignition and started to drive, Beth put her left hand on his right hand in a gentle way, but only for a moment, and said, "I wish that today was Friday instead of Thursday, Bob."

Garcia didn't immediately grasp her meaning, and asked, "Why?"

"Because then tomorrow would be Saturday," she replied with a soft smile, and a seductive glint in her eyes.

"Oh," he responded, "Guess I'm a little slow on the uptake," as he gave a warm smile in return. Then they drove the rest of the short distance to the shop in silence, forgetting the murder case for the moment. Both of them then thinking only about Saturday's date and what it might mean to their careers and to their personal lives.

FIFTEEN

Even before they parked the car the detectives saw that the antique shop was open; the lights were on, and since it was early evening it was easy to view the interior of the store and to note that no one was at the entrance or at the glass-topped counter. It all appeared to be very quiet; entering through the door, however, created some noise because the door was a trigger for a loud sounding bell, which was of course designed to alert Zach Segal that he had a visitor or a customer. As the detectives entered they were conscious of someone coming out of the back of the shop. It was Zach Segal, and he appeared to be slightly inebriated. He weaved slightly as he stepped forward to greet Reed and Garcia, viewing them only as possible customers. He made an honest effort to appear as sober as possible, an incongruous smile on his face.

"Good afternoon, folks; how can I help you?" he said in a slow deliberate drawl.

Detective Reed, deciding that she did not want to shake Segal's hand, just flashed her badge, as did Garcia, and said, "I am Detective Reed and this is Detective Garcia. We would like to ask you a few questions, assuming that you are Zach Segal."

Segal tried to get his wits together, straightened up a bit, and leaned forward on the glass counter as to steady himself. His first thought was of the scam he was working with Sam Meyers; could the police have any knowledge about that? How could they? He thought. He was finally able to answer Reed's question; "Yes, I'm Zach Segal, but why are you here? What kind of questions?" A few beads of perspiration appeared on his forehead, and his bleary eyes widened in fearful apprehension.

"We are investigating the murder of Dr. Richard Carnes, Mr. Segal, and our information is that he and you had a rather serious disagreement sometime ago, which we see as a possible justification for retaliation against the doctor. Is that true?"

Segal looked almost relieved when he learned of the reason for the detectives' visit, but then showed anger as he replied. "Yes, god-damn it, it was more than a disagreement; he screwed me out of $15,000. I sure as hell didn't kill him, but in no way can I say I'm sorry that someone did. Anyway, what difference does it make? According to the news reports, it seems that it was just a robbery that got out of hand; isn't that right?"

"That was just an early speculation, based on the first evaluation of the circumstances at the time. We now don't think that theory is correct. From what we have learned of the situation that developed between you and Dr. Carnes, we can understand your anger, Mr. Segal," Bob Garcia stated, "but we have to ask you some questions. To begin with, where were you last Saturday evening?"

Segal hesitated for a moment, acting as though he was trying to recall where he had been on that evening, but he was really trying to clear his head. He finally said, almost as though he was bragging, "I was with a prostitute at the Twilight Motel after an early dinner. Got back here about six or six thirty; then I was here going over my books and sucking on a bottle of Jack Daniels. I remember that I had some trouble with my bills file and wasn't paying attention to how much booze I had drunk until the whiskey was all gone. I was a bit under so I crapped out on a cot I have in the back room. I didn't wake up until Sunday morning, about seven-thirty."

Reed looked at the overweight, tipsy character in front of her, trying to picture him sleeping on a cot. Her experience and intuition told her that the man was lying, other than perhaps the admission that he was ticked off by Dr. Carnes and maybe about the prostitute. "We will check with the motel, of course, but it is the time you said you returned to the shop which needs some verification." She then asked, "I don't suppose you have any way to verify your being here last Saturday in the early evening, do you? If you took a cab from the motel, perhaps the cab driver could confirm the time that he dropped you off."

"No, I don't think so," Segal replied, acting more sober. "I drove here, parked at the back of the shop, but maybe one of the other tenants in this complex saw me, or at least might have seen some lights on."

"We'll make some inquires," Bob Garcia said. "We can check with the phone company and get verification of any calls that you may have made from here Saturday between say four o'clock and nine. That might validate your statement. Do you recall if you did make any phone calls that night?"

Segal shook his head as though trying to recall if he had made any calls, or he at least gave that impression, but he answered, "No; frankly I know that I had enough to drink that night that I could have, but I just don't remember."

"Are you married, or do you have a live-in partner?" Beth Reed asked. "If you are, maybe your wife or partner could confirm your being here Saturday night. It would be even better if you had someone unrelated to you, however it still might help if they were to provide some confirmation of your whereabouts that night."

"No, I'm not married, not anymore," Segal admitted. "I was, for awhile, but it was a disaster; I was not much of a husband. It was a good thing that we never had any children. I do have a friend that might have remembered I told her I had some book work to do last Saturday. I'll give her a call; if she remembers, I'll let you know, and you can talk to her."

"That will be fine, Mr. Segal; we'll check back with you on that. Now the nurse at the doctor's office could give us very little in terms of the financial transaction you and the doctor had entered into, so it would help us to have you fill in the blanks on that matter." Reed explained. "We have had a long day, and apparently you have had one too, so if you don't mind, we would like to have you sketch out the deal you had with the doctor and set it aside for us to pick up tomorrow sometime. Your door says your shop hours are from ten to six, so we'll come by while you're open tomorrow. A handwritten summary is all we need, just to have a confirmation of the transaction in our file. In fact, if you have a fax machine, or one is available to you, you could fax us that information at any time, 24/7. At the same time you can let us know about your friend's memory. If you have any questions as you prepare the transaction details, or anything else, here is my card, the Fax number is on it, and of course, you can call us anytime."

Garcia added, "Unless we have something else that comes up, we'll be back tomorrow if you aren't able to fax us that information. There may be the possibility we may ask you for a blood sample, some saliva, or have you furnish something from which we can extract your DNA. If so, our lab tech will call you to make an appointment."

Segal's fat face flushed and he stammered a bit, "Why? Why . . . do you need that? You must believe that I'm a suspect! That's crazy; I told you where I was last Saturday." He was very disturbed, as his brain whirled around with thoughts of Dr. Carnes, Sam Meyers, money, and Mrs. Elizabeth Gordon.

Detective Reed looked at him with a critical eye. She was happy to see him upset, thinking that in that condition he may blurt out something that could incriminate himself. "Mr. Segal, if you have nothing to worry about, just accept our requests as part of our job to clear you as a suspect, which is what we have to do with all of the people who have had an unhappy relationship with Dr. Carnes, as a patient or otherwise. You are just one of several people that we must investigate and clear as possible suspects. It is our objective to clear you as soon as possible, so we can pursue some of the other leads. We would expect you to notify us if you decide to take an extended trip anywhere, close your shop, or move your residence; do you understand? Ask us now if you have any questions about what we have discussed with you. If not, we will leave you now."

Segal was disturbed, but nodded his head in acceptance, "Of course I understand," he answered gruffly, "and I have no other questions, but he then gave the team a small wave as they left the shop. As soon as the detectives were out the door, he said out loud to no one "Shit!" then turned around to return to the back room, and the half bottle of Jack Daniels he had left in order to greet his visitors.

Back in their unmarked police car, the detectives pondered over the responses given by Zach Segal and questioned themselves as to whether he could be a legitimate suspect in the murder of Dr. Carnes. "I don't know why, but I believe Segal is lying about everything, except for his hatred of the doctor," Garcia stated.

Beth Reed voiced her own reaction to Zach Segal. "I have the same feeling, Bob, but if he is innocent, why should he lie? I'm inclined to think that he is hiding something; perhaps something that has nothing to do with the murder. I think that it's always harder to interrogate anyone that is even slightly under the influence. Anything that they say immediately becomes suspect as to whether what they say is the truth or a lie. That's our job, Bob, to sort out all the crap we hear."

"After meeting that character, I feel like I need a shower. On a happier note, it's pretty late in the day, Beth; why don't we call it a day and meet with Hobson tomorrow morning? We should bring him up to date on the case anyway. Oh hell; I forgot that he won't be back in the office until Monday."

"He said we could get in touch with him, if needed, but I don't think we have anything significant to report," Reed replied. "Hobson is probably right about blood being the most likely tie-in to the killer. He made it clear he is anxious for us to pursue obtaining court orders to require blood samples to generate DNA numbers for both Segal and LeBland, and anyone else we believe might be a suspect. We can't include everyone, but at least that way we won't waste any more time if we go in that direction. It wouldn't of course, exclude any one of them from having hired a hit man, which Miss Brooks could do as well. There's always the chance too, as someone said, that the killer could have cut himself during the commission of the crime. It's a long shot, but I just think it would be smart to at least get all of the DNA numbers we can in our file. Who knows?"

Garcia looked at his partner and said, "Well I'm glad that you and I, and the chief, all agree on the direction to take at this point. Having them each provide blood and or saliva samples will probably make them squirm a little, whether one of them is guilty or not. Why don't I go into the office tomorrow morning and arrange for the court orders, and you could call Nurse Whitcomb and see if we can meet with her about ten? Unless you call me on my cell phone to cancel, I could meet you there about that time. As a matter of fact, since the chief seems to be emphasizing the blood factor, I think that I will have the orders issued for all of the contacts we have had so far, and then call in to the legal department when we generate any new ones. That way I won't have to waste anymore time in that department. I'll also ask that the lab guys ask for permission from the persons being checked to remove any clothing or other objects that they want to inspect further; just to make it all legal. If anyone objects, we'll just have to get separate court orders for those situations."

"Good idea, Bob. You know I hate the paperwork part of this job; you do that and I'll call the clinic. I've been thinking about Nurse Whitcomb having to meet and work with the doctor's attorney. I know that she's not looking forward to working with him. It's a stretch, but we can't ignore the fact that he unquestionably has an interest in the resolution and dispensation of the clinic's assets, and I suspect that he may have somehow managed to actually obtain the power of attorney that would give him authority to control the whole liquidation. Let's forget work now though, Bob. If you don't mind, I'd like to have you drop me off at my apartment. For some reason I'm pooped; I think part of the reason for that is we're struggling to pinpoint a suspect we think could be the killer. I'm ready to kick off my shoes, have a shower and a glass of wine, prop my feet up on a big pillow and vegetate in front of the television. I'll probably fall asleep in my recliner."

"That sounds like a good plan for the evening," Garcia agreed. "I just might do the same thing, Beth, except for the wine. One more thing for you to know about me; I am a scotch drinker; prefer Dewars . . . at least before a dinner, maybe a little Merlot with the meal. But I'm not a nut about it; I'll drink whatever someone has available to serve; even gin or vodka, but not bourbon. I've even been known to drink water," he laughed. Bob drove Beth home and squeezed her left hand as she exited the car with a warm smile. It left him thinking more about Saturday night.

SIXTEEN

When Detective Bob Garcia walked into the office Friday morning the receptionist said, "Oh, Detective Garcia, I'm glad you came in; I've been trying to reach you or Detective Reed. A Charles Bingham has called twice to reach one of you. He wants you to call him as soon as you can." The receptionist handed Garcia a telephone call slip and said, "Here is his number, and he said that he expected to be home all day; if not, he said he has a recorder and you could leave a message as to when you could meet with him at his home."

Garcia accepted the call slip from the receptionist. "Thanks, Cindy; we were hoping to hear back from him. Don't bother to tell Detective Reed about this when she comes in; she should be here by about ten to meet with me and I'll give her the info. Were there any other messages? Has Chief Hobson called in since he's been gone?"

"There were no other messages for you or Detective Reed, at least not while I've been on the board, but my relief gal, Millie, said the chief had called in about an hour ago, and that he had talked to Detective Walters about an arson case involving some kind of commercial building; that's all. He didn't leave any messages for you or detective Reed; if he had, Millie would have put it on the message spindle."

Garcia thanked her and then went to the legal department and gave the details to a staff member to draw up the court orders for Brooks, Segal, and LeBland. As an afterthought, he also added Charles Bingham to the list, since the Lab tech would be right next door anyway; and as another second thought, he requested the law clerk leave the orders open so he or his partner could call in additional names, if necessary; explaining it would save them coming into headquarters again. He then also politely insisted the law clerk have his request filled as quickly as possible, in hopes a Lab assistant could still get to the various locations and obtain the blood samples before the weekend. He expected there would be a further delay to get the DNA work done, but the first step was to get the blood. Instructions were to be given to the Lab person to get a saliva sample for just the DNA testing if there was a problem in getting the blood. Fridays were not the best day to get special services done, but Bob Garcia was hopeful that by mentioning Senior Detective Reed's name in relation to the requests that it might trigger quicker responses. He wanted to have everything arranged for by ten o'clock, the time when he was to meet with Beth Reed. It took more time than he thought was necessary, but it was all set when Detective Reed walked into his station.

"Good morning, Bob; any trouble getting the court orders?" she asked, settling into Garcia's conference chair.

"I'm glad you got in so soon, Beth," Garcia replied. "You will be happy to hear it is all a project in motion, and we should have the court orders signed by one of the judges this afternoon, unless someone screws up; or they have a problem finding a judge that isn't in session. The law clerk, James Brock, said that Judge Kaplan was usually very considerate, and would even sign orders while he was on the bench, willing to hold up the procedures for a few minutes. I hope that you agree with me on this, but I asked that if there were any problems with the getting the blood samples, the tech person at least should get some saliva so we can get the Lab going on the DNA numbers. Now how about you, were you able to get in touch with Miss Brooks, and do we have an appointment?"

"Whoa partner, I think that's about three questions," Reed answered. "First of all, that was a smart move, Bob, about the saliva and the DNA; that really is the most important information we need right now. And, yes, I did finally get Marly Brooks on the phone. I tried several times to begin with, and was about ready to give up; when she finally answered the phone, she told me that she had been in the shower washing her hair, and said that she doesn't have a recorder. In any event, we are set to call on her this early afternoon, about one thirty; I was surprised that she didn't kick up a fuss about having another meeting with us. Whether she was putting on an act or not, at least she was pleasant with me over the phone."

"That's great, Beth; we may be able to kill two birds with one stone, as they say, because her neighbor, Charles Bingham, has been trying to reach us. He left two messages with the receptionist, she gave me the telephone slips as to the time, etc. when I came in, but I haven't tried to call him back. I couldn't make an appointment with him anyway, at least not until I knew what plans you may have made. Now that we have a time to meet Brooks, why don't we just pop in on him when we finish with his neighbor? Unless you think we should call first. As I said I would, Beth, I added him to the court order list, along with all of the others we have had contact with. That will probably be fruitless, but we at least are following the chief's thinking. I also just thought that as long as the tech was going to be at Brooks he might just as well go next door. I hope that you don't have any problem with my arranging that."

"Not at all, Bob; that's in line with our attempt to cover all bases. I think we'll gamble on his being there when we arrive. I want us to talk to Miss Brooks first, but I don't know how long we'll be with her. If he sees our car when we arrive, or when you park it, he will probably assume that we will walk next door when we're through with Brooks. In any event, we will meet Marly first." Senior Detective Reed took a deep breath and exhaled as though she was depressed. "Aren't you surprised, Bob, that we have not heard a word about anyone using those credit cards or that somehow Dr. Carnes' wallet has not turned up? It is sort of a side point, but the absence of those items, in a sense, further confirms it was not a crime of robbery. We don't need that confirmation, I know, after getting the forensics' report, but if those items were found they might help us determine the identity of the killer. I'm sure that is why they have intentionally not been used; if the killer had no financial use for them, I think we can forget trying to follow up that line of thinking. I would venture that he has destroyed them days ago."

"Actually, Beth, I have to admit I haven't given that subject much thought at all, but now that you mention it, it isn't all that surprising we haven't had any feedback on the credit cards or the wallet. I think you're right that the killer didn't even try to use those credit cards, so the only thing he might still have would be the wallet, and that was probably chucked into a dumpster after he took out the cash. Do you think that it would be worthwhile to have the sanitation department check the trash and garbage picked up from the homes of the three main suspects' homes this week? We're only talking about less than one week's refuse."

"That would really be a long shot, Bob, but who knows? I'll check with the receptionist and see if she can find out who we should talk to at the sanitation department, while you go back and see how they're doing with the court orders. If Cindy has the number and can get some manager on the phone, I might just see if I can arrange for some kind of search of the dump right then. If not, I'll call later. In either event, I'll wait for you at the reception area, and then we can head out to see Miss Brooks."

Garcia replied, "That's a good idea, Beth. If nothing else, by checking back with the legal department it might let them know about the urgency of our request. If I get delayed there, I'll call Cindy so she can let you know." He left Reed and proceeded to the legal department.

Cindy, the receptionist, was unable to get a representative of the sanitation department with any authority on the phone, but she did have the correct number for Reed to call and try later. Detective Reed had barely turned around from talking to Cindy when Bob Garcia walked up to her. "Any luck?" he asked.

"Unfortunately, no," Reed answered, "No one with any authority was available, but I have the number. I'll call later. Let's get on the road and see if Miss Brooks has anything more to say that will help us

SEVENTEEN

The detective team arrived at Marly Brooks home just five minutes before the scheduled meeting time and parked on the driveway side closest to Charles Bingham's house. They were hoping he might see them pull up and thereby expect to see them later, but he was nowhere in sight. They walked up the three wooden steps to the front porch of Brooks' little home, which was badly in need of a coat of paint or stain. In fact, the exterior of the entire house was in an obvious state of deterioration. It seemed almost ludicrous to the detectives that they should be calling on the particular occupant as someone who could possibly be involved in a murder . . . it all seemed too improbable. There was no sound from the doorbell that Garcia pushed twice, so Garcia used his knuckles and rapped hard enough to make sure Miss Brooks could hear them even if she was occupied in the back of the house. In a short minute, however, the woman opened the door.

Without any kind of a greeting, she merely said, "Come in," but then added that she was sorry to have kept them waiting.

Detective Reed forced a slight smile as she responded, "Thank you, Marly. We are sorry, too, to have to bother you again, but we have some information that we think you should have, and we may have to ask you another question or two." Detective Garcia nodded to Brooks as a matter of courtesy, as he followed Reed through the front door, and the three of them paraded through to the kitchen, where Miss Brooks pointed to two chairs around the small table, as she settled herself in a third.

"Frankly, I did not expect to see you back here again. You surely cannot consider me to be a suspect in the murder of Dr. Carnes, even though you know I hated the man for what he did do me," Brooks asserted. "What do you want of me, anyway?" She showed no anger, just a tone of impatience.

Detective Reed answered, "You are only one of several people who have had an unhappy relationship with the victim, Marly, and we are required, as we have said before, to fully investigate each and every one. Eventually, we will probably have several other individuals to consider as suspects we don't even know about at this time, so we are a long way from closing this case. In this work we often find that it is an associate or someone connected to one of the early suspects that end up doing the actual criminal act. We just can't completely clear anyone until we have all of the cold hard facts. You may find it surprising and objectionable, but one of the things we still need from you is a sample of your saliva and possibly your blood. We have requested court orders for blood and saliva samples from other persons so that we can obtain the DNA numbers. If the orders are prepared yet today, as we hope, you may have one of our Lab techs call on you later this afternoon. We hope you will understand the necessity for this action, and will give our tech person your full cooperation."

Detective Garcia interjected a comment and a question to Brooks, who sat with her head tilted, as though she was listening to something else. "Miss Brooks," Garcia said, to get her attention. "When we were here the first time it was apparent that you were somewhat distraught, and we thought it best to curtail our questioning of you, but there is one question that we must ask you, for the record. Did you have anything at all to do with the murder of Dr. Carnes?"

Marly looked a little startled, finding it hard to believe what she had heard. "Why of course not, how could I? She replied, rather disgustedly."

Garcia apologized, "I'm sorry Miss Brooks, but I must also ask if you know anyone else who may have had something to do with that murder?"

Again, Brooks was almost belligerent in her reply, emphatically stating, "No, for God's sake, I do not!"

Detective Reed picked up the interrogation: "You implied during our first meeting that you had no male friends or family with whom you associate; however, from what we do know about you, Miss Brooks, you emigrated from Ireland some years ago; so did any of your relatives follow you here? In other words, do you have any family members living in this vicinity?" Detective Reed asked.

Marly Brooks replied strongly, "No, I do not have any relatives living in this vicinity. Is that enough!" She asked categorically.

"I think that's all for now," Reed replied, "But please remember about our tech call sometime this afternoon. Thank you for your time. We will see ourselves out."

The two detectives rose and walked to the front door; Brooks stayed sitting at the kitchen table and said nothing more. Garcia closed the door behind them, saying to his partner, "I caught something in that last reply; did you?"

Beth Reed said, "Yes, I did, but we can talk about that later. Let's walk next door and see if our neighbor, Mr. Bingham is home."

As they proceeded toward the neighbor's home they saw that Bingham was already descending from his own porch to the front walk. This time he carried an artistically carved cane instead of the broom he had in his hands at their first visit. He wasn't limping, but walked slowly and did not look very strong. They greeted him part way down the walk. Detective Reed spoke first. "Thank you, Mr. Bingham, for your call. We received the message that you were trying to reach us, and we presumed that you may have learned something that will be of help in our investigation, which we can tell you now, is on the murder of Dr. Richard Carnes. We intentionally did not tell you that during our first visit, for a number of reasons. We suspect though, that you have learned that from the publicity being given this case."

Bingham responded, "I sort of thought that anyway; I just put two and two together. I heard from the news reports that Dr. Carnes had been killed, and I knew that Marly had worked for him. We talked about it every once in awhile over the years. We all knew that she blamed him for her disfigurement; he sure left her in a helluva condition. In any event, the reason I called is because she had a visitor the night before last. It was a man, the same one that I think I saw visit her before. I could only see him from a little distance away, but he parked his car this time at a perfect angle for me to be able to see his license plate from my little picture window. I wrote it down on this piece of paper," he said as he handed the sheet to Detective Reed. "You can see it is an out-of-state plate; Georgia." He seemed quite pleased with himself at being able to give the information to the detectives, but started to cough when he had finished, as though it had been an effort for him.

"That is really great," Garcia said in congratulating Bingham; "That is the type of cooperation we in law enforcement appreciate. Speaking of cooperation, since you are now really a part of our investigation, we are asking our Lab techs to get a blood sample from you, that or a saliva sample so that we will have DNA numbers for everyone that we have interviewed. It is just routine; hope you understand. We will follow up on the license plate lead right away, but please still keep our confidences to yourself, Mr. Bingham; we especially do not want to get the neighborhood all up in a tizzy and start speculating as to who, what, and why we're conducting this investigation."

"Oh I will keep mum, I will; you can bank on that, and I'll still keep an eye out for anything unusual going on next door, and I have no objection to the blood test." Bingham waved to the two detectives as he strode somewhat unsteadily back to his own front door.

"This is getting more and more interesting, Bob," Senior Detective Reed said to her partner. "Miss Brooks, as we both noted, thinks that she was cute the way she replied about the relative in the vicinity. Which I'm sure only made both of us think that she does have a relative in the states, but not in the vicinity. Her male visitor may or may not be a relative, but all that she has done in my mind is made herself look guilty . . . of something."

"Exactly the way I see it too, Beth. She may be a victim, but she is hiding something; it may not be Carnes' murder, but it could involve drugs or an immigration situation. I think that there is a part of her life that we know nothing about, at least at this point. Maybe I'm letting my imagination run a little wild, but I can't help but think that there are some secrets about Marly Brooks that we will learn about before this case is solved. Well why don't we call it a day, and start thinking about tomorrow night." He gave Beth a big grin as he made that comment.

Reed returned the smile and said, "Bright idea Bob; would you mind dropping me off at that drug store a half block from my apartment? I need a few things, and I can walk home from there. I need some exercise; we don't get much sitting in the car most of the day."

"It would be my pleasure, partner," Bob Garcia said; he then drove Beth Reed to the store. As they parted, they gave each other a hand squeeze, and Beth Reed leaned over and gave Bob Garcia a light cheek kiss before she left the car. No other words were necessary.

EIGHTEEN

At six o'clock sharp Saturday night, as they had prearranged, Detective Bob Garcia drove up to the apartment complex where Detective Beth Reed resided. He had talked to himself all the while he was driving from his own apartment, trying to calm himself down and get himself into the right psychological mood he felt that he would need to make the evening as enjoyable as possible. He tried the mental exercise of trying to think about Beth as a woman, a date, not his police woman partner. His hope was that they would generate a stronger, and closer personal relationship with each other. He didn't dare speculate for anything else beyond that; yet in the back of his mind he envisioned something more. Reed was waiting for Garcia in the small apartment lobby, and greeted him with a short hug, saying, "That's like I expected, Bob, right on time."

Garcia laughingly replied, "Well I didn't want to keep you waiting; I remembered the old adage . . . you never get a second chance to make a good first impression." They both chuckled at that, and Garcia didn't give Beth a chance to respond. Bob spoke again as he held the door open for Beth. "I also wanted to enjoy every minute of our time together tonight. And I'm also hoping that it will be enjoyable for you. We have a reservation at John's Steak House at six-thirty, but don't worry if you aren't into steaks. They have a pretty wide selection of entrees' on their menu, including both fish and pasta, but no Chinese."

"It sounds exciting already," Beth expressed with some warm enthusiasm. "I eat almost everything, and I love good food, but I just don't eat large quantities. My folks and my three siblings were all big eaters, and they became big people, but I swore that I would never make eating a big thing in my life. It hasn't been easy with the genetic background that I have."

As they walked to the car, Bob said, with an admiring twinkle in his eye, "Well your self control shows in your body, which incidentally looks terrific in that beautiful blue dress; quite different from your professional white blouse and black slacks; it matches your eyes. And I can't believe how great you look, too, with your hair down instead of that official policewoman's hair bun, and I don't think that I have ever seen you with any makeup; wow!" Beth gave Garcia one of her happiest smiles as she entered his car.

When they entered John's Steak House, Garcia asked the hostess if they could have a corner booth, saying to Reed, "If that's alright with you."

Beth confirmed with a nod that that was just fine with her, and the hostess led them to a booth that was a little ways away from the major dining area, having sensed that the couple sought some degree of privacy. Before they were seated, Beth asked Bob, "Would you mind if we sat cattycorner rather than across from each other, or next to each other? I think that it's a cozier arrangement, and makes it a bit more private. Sitting the other ways seems awkward to me for just two people. Face to face is like a business dinner, and that isn't what I think we have in mind." She laughed.

"There you go, Beth, reading my mind again. That is really why I asked for a corner booth. I'm going to have to be careful what I am thinking if you're going to be reading my mind!" he exclaimed, as they both gave out a nervous laugh.

When the waiter approached and handed them menus, Bob asked Beth what she would like to drink before dinner; "White wine would be fine, Chardonnay, preferably," she indicated. The waiter heard, nodded, and noted the order on his pad.

"I'll have Dewars and water, with a twist of lemon," Bob requested. He then turned to Beth and explained, "As I think I mentioned awhile back, I like to have a scotch before dinner, but then I'll usually have some red wine with my dinner. That is the first peculiarity about me that you have learned; I have more."

The drinks were delivered, and the menus were set aside as Garcia told the waiter they were in no hurry and that they would order later. He then raised his glass of scotch and proposed a toast: "Here's to the beginning of an adventure into the unknown; who knows what may be discovered?"

"Wow! That sounds pretty heavy for a plain old detective; do you have many other talents that I don't know about?" Beth asked, rather impressed with Bob's toast. They clinked glasses and then sipped their drinks, with Beth looking into Bob's eyes in genuine admiration. As cheerful as she looked, what with her black hair neatly down to her shoulders, it would be difficult for anyone to guess she was a detective.

Bob put his glass down and asked Beth, "This is probably an unlikely question to ask on a first date, Beth, and I hope you don't mind my asking, but I have wondered, ever since they paired us up, how and why an attractive woman like you would choose police work as a career."

"That's pretty easy to answer, Bob, and I don't mind your asking at all. First of all being an Irishman in New York City, my father found the career as a policeman was the best he could obtain to provide a decent income for his family in accord with the limited education he had. He did attend night school for awhile, in hopes of becoming a lawyer, but his big family required too much time. One of my brothers, the oldest one, also became a policeman, but never got advanced to detective work. You might say it was in our blood. I had two years of college before I got married, stopped going to school because I wanted to become a mother. Back then my family all thought differently than young people think today; they believed that a mother should stay home and raise the family. Well as I have said before, it all didn't quite work out that way. But I have really enjoyed my career; I made it to detective partly because I did have that two years of college, and my intended major was police administration. I got frustrated with the politics of the New York Police Department and left by myself when I was able to get on the force in Tallahassee; I worked my way over to Orange Grove about two years later. What about you, Bob, how and why are you in police work? And I hope you don't mind my asking," she laughed.

"Of course not," Bob responded. "When I was a teenager my favorite uncle was a policeman, not Irish of course," Garcia laughed, "But he wasn't one very long, he was gunned down by some punks who he tried to stop as they were robbing a fast-food restaurant. As a kid, somehow I felt that I should avenge his death, so here I am. Sometimes though, I feel that it is a lost cause. The young people today have no respect for policemen, or for teachers, or even their own parents. I don't know where we are going because in many ways we are not even a civilized country. Certainly not according to what my uncle used to say, which was: "Being civilized means doing what you need to do, or what you want to do, within the law and without causing injury, discomfort, or harm to anyone." I thought he was a very smart man; he was sort of a philosopher. I remember too, how he also condemned movies and television shows for providing what they call entertainment, but in fact it is just profiteering from every uncivilized action they can think of to portray, with a way over emphasis on sex. I'm sorry, Beth, this doesn't sound like a first great date for anyone. Let's order our meal and talk about more pleasant things . . . like you."

"I don't know about that," she grinned. "I've always been too serious for most of my life. I do enjoy a good joke, sexy or otherwise, but I don't like it when some comediennes poke fun at the Irish, Poles, Jews, or any other ethnic group in a way that is not funny to those very people. My dad was very sensitive to that kind of humor; I suppose it was because his parents migrated from Ireland; I think that it was during the great potato famine. And all that had nothing to do with religion; in fact they were what we call "people persons." They had their own philosophy, which was: "the only spirit that matters is that which exists between people." However, they brought us up to respect all religions, and the family has a lot of mixed marriages, but fortunately no language problems."

Detective Bob Garcia began to see his partner in an entirely different light; she had easily put aside her strong role as a detective, and he was glad to learn that religious differences would not be a problem for them. He saw Beth as a very attractive woman, one that he began to feel a desire for; her checks had been delicately reddened, her sparkling blue eyes had a brightness that he had not seen before, and her hair was not in a bun behind her head, but swirled down in a teasing way. He was sitting to her left and he put his right arm around her shoulders and pulled her up against himself. He was five-eleven and she was near five-nine; she looked up at him, her eyes met his in an understanding way. Without saying a word, Bob took his left hand and raised Beth's lips to his own. It was a quiet kiss, but was not brief. When they broke, she said, "Well I guess that changes the conversation," and they both laughed and exhaled at the same time. "But," she went on, "You better take your napkin to your red lips," she laughed again.

The meal was very satisfying, the wine was good, and the conversation was both intimate and exhilarating, but when Garcia took Beth Reed back to her apartment, she did not invite him in. She did, however, permit him some liberties that left him rather excited, including a lingering, wet kiss they would both be thinking about when they settled themselves in bed that night. Neither felt than anything more had to be said as they parted, and both knew this evening was not the end, only the beginning.

It was a trying weekend for both of them as each of them thought several times about calling the other; Bob especially, but he didn't want to be too aggressive, too soon. They both thought about how they would feel when they reunited in the office on Monday morning, and how they would act when alone in the police car. They each had many considerations to mull over until then, not the least of which was the hope that they would be able to continue to be partners. There would be some challenges ahead, they knew that, but inside they had new warmth in their lives, and they were happy.

NINETEEN

Monday morning found the detective team at headquarters, each seated at their individual stations, poring over their notes on the Carnes murder, and trying not to glance over to the other's area. Beth Reed made the first move and walked over to Garcia's cubicle with some papers in her hand. He started to rise as she approached, but Reed discreetly motioned with her other hand, sort of patting the air, which Garcia understood meant that he should remain seated. She had only a hint of a smile on her face, which matched the smile that she would have given anyone, any morning. It was evident to Garcia that she did not want to express any unusually warm greeting that might be interpreted by others in the office to mean that something else was going on. He responded in a like manner, saying coolly, "It looks like you've got our schedule for the day all set partner; right?"

"Well, somewhat," Beth Reed answered. "I haven't heard if the lab guys were able to execute the court orders Friday afternoon. Even if they did get all of the samples we requested, it will probably be Wednesday or so before they can give us the blood and DNA numbers we need. I think that the first thing we have to do this morning is talk to the Department of Motor Vehicles and see if they can get information from Georgia as to who owns the car spotted by Mr. Bingham."

"I thought about that Friday afternoon when we left Mr. Bingham, but then it dropped out of my mind." Garcia said with a straight face. "For some reason, or another."

Detective Reed looked knowingly at her partner, but was thinking more like the detective that she was, putting her concerns of the Carnes murder before anything else.

"I know that what I'm going to say may sound strange, Bob, but I have learned from the past that if I get a gut feeling about something I have to follow through with it, even though it may turn out to be a dead end. I think that we missed a point in our questioning of Marly Brooks. I know that she is obviously not living high on the hog, but she is, never the less, sustaining herself. Where is the income coming from that she needs to just exist? We made some assumptions about her being classified as being totally disabled under Social Security, but we don't really know that. I suggest that you call DMV about the Georgia plate and I'll call Brooks and set up a time to see her this morning. Go check with Cindy or whoever is manning the receptionist's desk, about the number we need to call. Maybe she can get the right party for you herself and you can take the call at your desk. In any event, walk over to my station after you finish with the DMV folks and then we'll leave for Brooks place, if she if available."

"I'm sorry, Beth, I can't see where that is going to help lead us to Dr. Carne's killer. I thought we had pretty much dismissed Brooks as not being directly involved with the murder. It doesn't seem to me that she has the money, any kind of a friend, or anything else that would make a connection for us." Garcia questioned. "I know we have to learn more about her mysterious visitor, and admittedly there may be some kind of connection there, but it would really be a reach. I don't know, maybe I'm being too skeptical."

"No, it's alright; your questioning my thinking is okay, Bob, I expected it; as I said in so many words, my gut feeling is strange, and is probably way off center, but I just have to go with it. I can't help but feel that there is another candidate somewhere that committed the actual crime, but I think that that person is more connected to Marly Brooks than they are to either Zach Segal or Mr. LeBland. As partners, it would be surprising if at times we did not have some opposing opinions. If we didn't have different opinions from time to time, our partnership would be boring," They both laughed, and then Reed paused to see if her partner had anything else to say about the direction of their murder investigation.

Garcia hesitated to say anything more; after all here was his "boss" and the woman he had begun to have strong feelings for; he also respected her judgment and was aware of the fact that she was much more experienced than he was. "Okay," he agreed, "I'll get in touch with someone at the DMV, probably through Cindy, and I'll stay at my station until you come back here and let me know if we're going to go see Brooks today. The blood and DNA numbers won't help us much when we get them if the killer is someone we still haven't identified."

"I know, Bob, but this case seems to have so many different directions for us to follow, I want to eliminate them one at a time so we don't waste any more time chasing bad leads. This visit may put an end to Marly Brooks as someone involved with the crime, or it may put us on the right path. Okay, partner?" Reed asked, and gave Garcia a smile to which he could only give his consent.

He smiled back, and said, "Of course; we're a team; I think that we'll solve this damn murder together, and soon. I'll wait for you here Beth; go make your call to Miss Brooks."

Cindy had been able to get the right number at the DMV office and got the supervisor at the Jacksonville DMV office on the phone for Detective Garcia, then buzzed him on the intercom to pick up the phone. Jim Carroll, the supervisor, had some information for his caller. "Well Detective Garcia, we may have a lead for you here on the case you discussed with me, because the number you gave us has been traced to a Sean McCoy, a pool hustler in Brunswick, Georgia. He does have a record, but only for petty theft, nothing much else."

"Brunswick? Where the devil is that?" Garcia asked.

"Just north of Jacksonville, actually; right on the coast," Carroll replied. "It's not a very big city, more of a town, but it gets its' share of the tourist trade, and I think that they do a lot of deep sea fishing from there. I visited there once, a couple of years ago, and I know that their climate is not unlike our own here in Jacksonville, which unfortunately makes it great for beach bums; they have their share of those, as we do."

"Would you do us another favor, Jim, and send our office a fax on the name, address, and physical description of McCoy? There may be a connection with him and a Miss Marly Brooks who is a principal involved in the murder of Dr. Richard Carnes."

"No problem, Bob; I'll have someone get that off to you in the next fifteen minutes, if not sooner. We had heard about that case up here even before you contacted us; Orange Grove is only a hundred miles or so west of us. Nice little city." Carroll commented. Garcia thanked Carroll and hung up. Just a few minutes later, Beth Reed walked into his station.

"Any luck Bob?" she asked immediately, maintaining her "official" posture.

Detective Garcia went with the flow and quickly answered her question. "As a matter of fact, partner, we may have gotten some help from Jacksonville. The head guy at their DMV office, Jim Carroll, is having someone in his office fax us the name, address, and description of the owner of the car, according to the plate number Bingham gave us. An interesting thing is that his name, if he was the one driving the car, is Sean McCoy. To me that indicates that he could be related to our Irish Miss Brooks, even though they have different surnames. Or, of course, he might just be a family friend from overseas. Jim Carroll voluntarily did check with the Brunswick police department to see if Sean McCoy had a record; he did have, but it was just for some kind of petty theft, nothing else."

"That <u>is</u> interesting, Bob; as soon as we receive that fax we can take it with us and it should provide an opening for discussing it with Miss Brooks. It might be the key to get her to tell us some meaningful information; I swear that she is holding back some things that we should know, that we may learn this afternoon. She was not very happy to hear from us again, but she did agree to see us anytime we get there today. We're not locked into an exact time, so we can just go as soon as we get the fax." Beth Reed seemed a bit relaxed and gave Garcia a warm smile, and he responded with one of his own. The faxed report came and Reed took it in her hand and said, "Let's go; I'll read it to you on the way." And the team left to see Miss Marly Brooks.

TWENTY

As they walked up to the little "cottage" they were surprised to be greeted right at the door by a less than friendly face, that of Marly Brooks; she then immediately challenged them with a question: "When are you guys going to start leaving me alone? By now you can't really expect that there is anything else I know that will help you in the investigation of Dr. Carne's murder." In spite of her vitriolic greeting, Marly Brooks unexpectantly invited the detectives into her home, and surprised them by actually suggesting that they sit at chairs around the little white kitchen table, which they did.

Senior Detective Beth Reed wasted no time with any niceties, however; instead she jumped right in with a question in connection with their last visit. "When we met with you previously, Marly, you stated that you did <u>not</u> have any relatives living in the vicinity, but we have reason to believe that you may have a relative in this country who is not in <u>this</u> particular vicinity, but who is actually not all that far away. Is that a true statement, or is there an explanation for what I have just said? Are you being evasive, or did you just not think about what you said previously?"

Miss Brooks looked sideways at Reed and then at Garcia, hesitating to respond to the question, then slowly admitted, "Yes, yes, I do have an older, half-brother, who visits me once in awhile, but I hardly think of him as a relative. He is not someone that I am proud to be related to, and he has not been of any help to me. From the little he has said about the jobs he has had, he has trouble making his own living. I just didn't want to bring him into this situation. He does check on me now and then since we have made contact. He told me that he writes the family back home to let them know how I am doing; I'm not sure about the truth of that. I never get any money from him or from what's left of my relatives over there. Sean has told me that everyone in Ireland that he is in touch with is as bad off as I am, so they haven't anything to send me. Sean said that he has informed them that I am on total disability under Social Security, so I guess they think that I'm okay financially. They have no idea about the cost of living over here. I don't think that they really understand what has happened to me, or what kind of life I have . . . or don't have. I would write to some of them, but I know that my letters would be too depressing; besides that, they have their own problems."

Detective Garcia interrupted Marly to ask, "Is the person that you are speaking about, Sean McCoy, and does he live in Brunswick, Georgia?"

"Yes, that's my brother; I believe that he has a small apartment in Brunswick. Obviously we do not even have the same name. His mother was my father's first wife. Between the two family groups, we have two brothers and a sister, but he is the only other one from the family, besides me, that came to the United States, and he has not been here very long. How did you find out about him? Who gave you his name?" Marly asked.

"I'm sorry, Miss Brooks, we can't reveal that," Beth Reed answered, "but we can tell you that it will be necessary to obtain blood and saliva samples from him and establish his DNA because we have to determine whether he is a suspect in this case, or if we have to clear him. It may be necessary for us to have a court order issued to obtain those samples through the Georgia authorities, unless you contact him and he steps forward voluntarily to do so himself. We would prefer that he drive into Florida and check in with the police department in Jacksonville, whom we will alert as to his arriving there, should he choose to comply. We would rather not involve the Georgia police in a Florida crime any more than we have to."

"The sixty four dollar question, Marly," Garcia interjected, "is, do you know where Sean was the Saturday evening of September the fourth, the night of the murder?"

"No, I don't!" Brooks angrily responded, "How the hell would I know; in the first place, I don't see why he has to be investigated; I rarely see him and he doesn't even live close by. Is it because he has some kind of police record? As far as I know it wasn't for anything serious, just shoplifting or something like that. I think that the incident happened before he was able to find some kind of job. I never found out how he was cleared to get into the country; I don't think that he wanted me to know; I assumed that he came in legally. He did tell me that he's never been in jail, but I'm not sure about that."

Reed and Garcia were both surprised at the strong objections by Brooks about their interest in her half-brother, thinking that there had to be a reason for it. On the other hand, they realized it could just be a sign of loyalty or concern for the only family member she had nearby. Reed did feel the need to comment, however, and said, "His record has nothing to do with our investigation, Marly, we are just doing our job. We're trying to solve a crime of murder, and until we clear all of the principals involved and find the killer, we can't afford to miss anything, and stepping on some toes at times cannot be avoided"

That seemed to settle Brooks down a little, but she still was somewhat agitated.

"Well I gave your blasted lab guys their samples, so maybe you'll clear me and I won't be bothered by you anymore."

"We can't promise you that, Miss Brooks," Reed stated, "although at this point it does look like you should be in the clear. We do have a number of other leads we have to follow which show more promise. We may have told you this before, but you have to realize that it may be necessary to have you testify in court as to the situation that developed between you and Dr. Richard Carnes. It all depends on how the case is finalized and who we charge with the crime. We're not prepared to make any commitments at this point in terms of what will be legally required by any of the persons involved in this investigation, or to excuse anyone."

"If you talk to your brother, you can tell him what we have said to you about what we want him to do," Detective Garcia instructed Brooks, "We will, of course, be following protocol to inform him anyway. You have our phone number, so please call us if there is a problem with him, or if you have any questions. Incidentally, does your brother wear a hat or cap?"

"Yes, of course. He wears a dark green tam, but not at work. I think that he does some kind of construction work; I don't think that he even owns a white shirt or a tie. What does that have to do with anything?" Brooks asked.

"Oh, I'm sorry Marly," Beth Reed said to Brooks, "Again, as I have said, I can't give you answers to your questions at this time, but I have to ask you two more questions. Do you have any personal contact with your neighbor, Charles Bingham?"

Still annoyed, Marly answered, "No, very little. Why do you ask? I don't understand why he would be relevant to your investigation. He's single; I know that his wife died a few years after I moved here. He was pretty healthy then and weighed over two hundred pounds, but it is obvious that he is not in very good health now. We don't talk to each other very much, but from a distance it looks to me like he may have cancer. I suspect that he may be worse off than I am. I hope that you don't have to give him a bad time too. So what is your other question?"

"I presume, since you don't go out very often, that you have your Social Security check direct deposited into a bank account; is that correct?" Detective Reed asked.

Miss Brooks gritted her teeth, getting the feeling that the "interview" was not going to end, and replied, "Yes, the Chase Bank in downtown Orange Grove, but I rarely go there because I don't drive. If I have any business with them it's usually by mail, or once in awhile I'll go into the bank for cash, or cash a check some place else; I don't have a credit or debit card." She gave a bitter laugh as she said, "I never get any offers to have one; it's okay though, because I can't afford to get into debt anyway."

"Is there anything particular about your financial affairs that you think we should know? Like are you the only person on your checking account, and is there a beneficiary named on it?" Reed questioned Brooks.

"No, no, to both of your questions," Marly stiffly replied.

"Well you should know that we will be confirming what you have told us with the Chase Bank," Detective Reed advised the woman. "We'll call you if there are any questions we have on the account. If you think of anything that might help us solve the murder, please call us. Thank you for your time," Reed said, without answering Brooks' question about why they were interested in knowing about her neighbor, and the team gathered their notes and left the kitchen table to walk to the front door, not fully accepting the explanation about her half-brother, Sean McCoy. Miss Brooks rose with them and preceded them to the front of the house. Reed and Garcia merely nodded to Marly as the team exited the little house.

Miss Brooks stood by the open door, looking after them with a look of mixed perplexity and anger on her face.

TWENTY ONE

Chief Detective Clyde Hobson was sitting at his desk poring over a pile of papers when his secretary, Marcia, buzzed him to let him know that if he was available, one of his investigators wished to see him; she was aware of which detectives had been assigned to the Carnes' case and informed the chief that the visitor was neither Reed or Garcia, but that it was Detective Roger Abbott. Hobson rose and greeted the man.

"Good to see you again, Roger," Hobson said, as they shook hands. "We haven't had much contact lately so this must mean that you have some info for me on one of our other cases; meaning other than the Carnes' murder. That right?"

"Yes and no, chief; however, there may be a tie-in," Abbott replied.

"That sounds interesting; how does it connect?"

"Well," Detective Abbot responded, "station 23 reported this morning that they got a call from a Mrs. Elizabeth Gordon, an upstanding, well-to-do woman who is married to State Representative Webb Gordon, and it appears that she almost became the victim of a jewelry scam."

The chief said, "I know Webb, we've played golf together several times; good golfer. I've met his wife too; she is a charming woman. What do you mean by she almost became a victim?"

"She must be a pretty smart woman," Abbott acknowledged, "because she recognized that the deal she was supposed to make was too good to be true, and got suspicious; unlike a lot of people who bite on those scams that are just too good to pass up. She said that at first it sounded like a good opportunity to buy some good jewelry pieces, particularly because she had been a customer of the Auld Lang Syne antique shop, and had confidence in the owner. She said that she had been looking for anniversary presents for her two daughters, and had been happy with the thought that she had found an answer to her shopping problem. She played along with the owner, the man who tried to screw her out of twenty-five grand, until she was able to call the local precinct, the 23rd, and get someone out to nab this guy."

"So how was the scam supposed to work; was the con guy the owner, or someone else that worked there, and how does all this work toward it being connected to the Carnes' murder?" Hobson asked Abbott.

"I am working on this fraud case with my partner, Carl Ingram, and we haven't got all of the facts clear yet, but we are quite sure that there are two men involved in the scam. The one that we collared and is now in the holding pen is the owner, as far as we know, of the antique shop, Zach Segal," Abbott reported. "I heard from one of the other boys that he is involved in the Carnes' case somehow; that's why I thought you'd be interested. Is that correct?"

Hobson combed his thick mustache with his fingers, a sign that he was mulling over a response, but then confirmed the situation, "Well that is a surprising coincidence Roger; yeah, he is one of the possible suspects that Reed and Garcia are investigating because he was a former patient of the doctor. They have kept me pretty well informed on the progress of the Carnes' case, so I'm sure they know nothing about a scam involving Mr. Segal; I would have heard about it. That will be another crazy thing for them to digest, in this crazy murder case they are working on. They've also given me the impression that they don't think that Segal murdered Carnes, but if he has an accomplice in a scam, the other guy might have done the dirty work for Segal. Get Mr. Segal on a chair in the interrogation room and see if you can squeeze out the name of his cohort. If you do get it, either get in touch with Reed and Garcia, or call me and I'll have them check the guy out. We already have the blood and saliva samples on Segal, and probably also have his DNA by now. I swear, every time I turn around there's a new angle on this case. Anytime now I expect to hear that maybe his barber did in Dr. Carnes. But tell me a little more, Roger, about the scam; we haven't had anything like a jewelry rip-off for a long while."

Detective Abbott explained how the scam was supposed to work, the forgeries of fake appraisals, the pictures of the jewelry, and the apparent honesty of Segal, owner of the antique shop, all of which gave him credibility, until Mrs. Gordon's antenna went up and she realized that the deal was too good to be true. "Luckily," Abbott said, "she was smart enough to hold on to the appraisals and pictures by telling Segal that she had forgotten that she had a hair appointment, had to leave for a little while, but that she would be back in an hour. Which, she said, would give her time to pick out the items she might buy while she was getting her hair done. Segal bought the story; in the meantime she called the precinct and she met their guys at the shop. Segal was alone and didn't offer any resistance after Mrs. Gordon revealed the scam in front of him and the arresting police officers. There was no way he could explain to them that it was a legitimate transaction; he just caved in."

Hobson nodded in acceptance of the charade, and said, "Well Mrs. Gordon may have helped us on two cases. Under the circumstances, I better alert the prosecutor's office to request that no bail be set for Segal because of the possible tie-in with the Carnes' murder. On second thought, I'll call Reed and Garcia right after you leave and at least let them know what's going on, but you still call them right away if Segal gives up the name of his accomplice."

"If Segal asks for an attorney, are we under any obligation to inform the lawyer that Segal is also a suspect in the Dr. Carnes's case?" Abbott inquired.

"No, we don't have to tell him, but I'm pretty sure that point will come up at the arraignment when bail will be asked to be denied by the prosecutor's office. Segal's lawyer, if he gets one, will be sure to question why bail should be denied, and the judge will have to tell him that it is because of Segal's being a suspect in a murder case. Of course someone else may tell him; I don't care, I just don't want Segal running free to skip the state or the country, at least until we sort out some of the details on the two cases and we know how they connect, especially because we now know that Segal had an accomplice in the scam. You might arrange to have a copy of your report on the scam given to either Reed or Garcia."

Abbott said, "Okay, boss, I'll take care of that myself," and left.

Hobson called his secretary on the intercom line and asked her to contact the Detectives Reed and Garcia and have them come in the next morning at nine o'clock for a review of the case in progress on the murder of Dr. Carnes, subject to any conflict that they might have. If there is one, then she was instructed to set another meeting ASAP, according to his own schedule of appointments. She was able to contact the detective team, learn that there were no conflicts, and set the meeting as Hobson had requested.

TWENTY TWO

The detective team had not been informed as to what the meeting was all about, other than they suspected that it was in regard to the case that had been assigned to them; the meeting had been set up on an unusually short notice. As requested, they appeared at the office of Chief Detective Clyde Hobson at exactly nine o'clock. While they were being seated in the two conference chairs facing the chief's desk, Marcia asked if they would like to have some coffee, which they accepted; they thanked her and she left after serving them. Chief Hobson was a bit more relaxed than he had been previously, and joined them with his own cup of coffee.

"It seems to me," he began, "that this Carnes case is getting more twists and turns that I ever expected, and I'm admittedly getting confused as to what direction we should be taking; we really_meaning you two. However, before we get into the details of what you have found and have concluded thus far, let me tell you about the latest twist, which, by the way, came from an unexpected direction. And I also have some interesting news from the Lab that we may find useful later on. Hobson then related the information that was given to him by Detective Roger Abbott and the arrest of Zach Segal for trying to scam a customer of his from the Auld Lange Syne antique shop. He also informed them that Segal was scheduled for arraignment, and where the prosecutor was expected to ask the judge to deny bail because of Segal's involvement with the Carnes murder.

"Wow!" Beth Reed exclaimed, "I can't believe Segal would stick out his neck on a scam when he still hasn't been cleared on the murder case. That's just plain dumb. On the other hand it is not entirely surprising, because both Bob and I feel that he has a serious drinking problem. Has he made any admissions on either case that would help convict him?"

"No, not yet," Hobson answered, "but Abbott is to put him through a tough interrogation, and I wouldn't be surprised if he came through with some facts that would help out on your case. However, the woman that was to be the scam victim told Abbott and his partner that she was sure that another man was involved. The other man might well be the killer that did the dirty work for Segal in getting his revenge on Dr. Carnes. At least we have to look at that scenario as a possibility. Roger Abbott hopes to get the name of Segal's accomplice out of him during the interrogation. Segal may have had to pull off the scam to get the money to pay his accomplice for the job. We don't know much about his financial situation, except as everybody knows, the antique business has plummeted since the recession, so he could be hurting. The public is not buying collectibles or antiques right now, so I'm sure that his income has dropped a lot."

"Well that is a strange thing to have happened," Beth Reed acknowledged, "Now let me tell you what <u>we</u> have learned. Our young Miss Brooks has admitted that she has a half brother living in a small town on the Georgia east coast who has visited her from time to time, and get <u>this</u>, he is also from Ireland and wears a <u>tam</u>. We're arranging to get a blood sample or saliva from him to obtain his DNA. The idea is to also eventually have our lab guys to also check the clothing of all of the suspects for blood specks. If the killer got hit with any substantial blood spatters, or even a drop or two, he would have gotten rid of the stained shirt or whatever, or had it laundered, but he may not have detected some spots and the garment might still be in his closet or laundry basket. It probably is somewhat unimportant, but the half-brother has a record for some minor offenses, something like shoplifting. He could have already committed some more serious offenses that have not been revealed, but in our minds that indicates that he probably has the potential for more than just petty theft."

Detective Garcia gave his partner a breather and continued with what they had learned. "It has been clear to us, chief, that Marly Brooks, though definitely physically impaired, is not a wholly truthful person. She has played games with us on the issue of her having any family members in the vicinity, and we have reason to believe that she has been getting some financial assistance from someone. She denies that she benefits from any help from her family in Ireland, but did admit to being on total disability under Social Security. We intend to analyze the activity that she has had in her bank account, which she has also confirmed as being at the main Chase Bank in downtown Orange Grove."

Detective Reed asked the Chief Detective, "Clyde, could you push on the lab work for us? I think that before any more time goes by, we should get that check of the clothing of all of the principals involved inspected for blood specks. We can give you the necessary info on Sean McCoy, the half-brother in Georgia. I agree with you in that we have been getting a lot of twists and turns in this case; that's one of the reasons Bob and I are anxious to get some of the suspects excluded. We know we need to concentrate on getting the evidence the prosecutor needs to convict the guilty person, or persons, but we just haven't been able to pinpoint that person. Oh, and what about that bit of news from the Lab that you said you did have?"

"I think that we are all getting pretty antsy about moving this case along, Beth," Hobson concurred. "If you give me the data on McCoy I'll ask to have a team from the Lab conduct those examinations immediately. As soon as I get the reports I'll have you two come in and we'll plan some follow-up procedures. As to that bit of news from the Lab . . . it may or may not be a key, but they reported finding two small spots of blood on Dr. Carnes clothing which do not match his own blood type. It could be meaningful if we find that it matches the blood type of one of our suspects.

We'll see. Things seem to be narrowing down, even though we have unintentionally widened the investigation. I've been fortunate that the top brass has been out of town at a convention in Miami; it has given me an enjoyable respite from their calls. I know that they are just doing their jobs, just like I have to do, but sometimes it is a little too much. Which makes me think about you two. You have both been on the go a lot with this case, and I know its' been frustrating for you, so why don't you also take a break while we wait for the lab work. The day is about shot anyway, but take a look at your mail and notes that someone may have left for you before you go, then enjoy the rest of the day. Maybe take in a movie, or watch one at home. I don't want either of you to get depressed over the lack of progress on this Carne's case."

Beth Reed exchanged glances with her partner, Bob Garcia, gave him a slight smile, and said to their boss, somewhat slyly, "That's very thoughtful of you, Clyde; I don't know about Bob, but that will give me a chance to catch up on my laundry and write a few letters to some of my family back in New York. Thanks again, boss . . . we're gone." And the team left with big grins on their faces. Detective Garcia saluted his chief as they left his office.

As they walked into the lobby area, Bob asked his partner, with a glint in his eye, "If you are reading my mind again, you have to have the same thought that I have. At least I hope that you do."

Reed looked around to assure herself that no one was within earshot, and quietly replied, in an uninhibited flirtatious way, "Dinner out, or a drink at my place and I thaw out a pizza while we relax? I picked up a bottle of scotch yesterday . . . just in case. Like you, I always try to be prepared," she laughed.

"That sounds like an invitation I can't refuse," Bob Garcia answered. "I am ready for that scotch . . . and anything else you might want to offer. Why don't you go on ahead; I need to make a stop at the drug store, now that you have subtly reminded me. As you said, just in case." They both chuckled.

They exited the office building, entered their own vehicles and left the parking lot at the same time. Detective Garcia made his stop at the drug store, spent some time browsing the magazine rack to give Reed a chance to freshen up before he got to her apartment, then proceeded on his way there. She opened the door at his knock, dressed in a silky, stay-at-home gown, her dark hair provocatively draped over her lightly covered breasts, and greeted her partner with a brief, but sensuous kiss, planted squarely on his eager mouth. Their eyes reflected the joy and excitement the kiss had generated.

"I've already poured myself some wine, Bob," Beth announced, and I would have had your drink ready, but I didn't remember how you like your scotch. I thought that you had it with just plain water when we had our dinner out, but I wasn't sure."

"Just plain water is right, Beth, and a fifty-fifty mix would be just perfect," Garcia responded. While Reed fixed his drink, Garcia removed his jacket and shoes and sat relaxed on one end of the little sofa in the all-purpose room, a casual non-traditional type of living room. "You have your place so pleasantly decorated, Beth, that I feel right at home. You may have trouble getting me to leave."

"Now don't get too comfortable, I wouldn't want you to fall asleep, at least not until later." Beth smiled enticingly as she returned with Bob's drink, then carefully handed it to him with her left hand while picking up her glass of wine from the marble covered coffee table. They clinked glasses as Beth settled into the sofa next to Bob.

He looked into her eyes and said, "Well Beth, we are embarking on a new adventure, and perhaps a risky one, but I hope that you feel as happy about it as I do.

Honestly, I can't believe how happy I feel inside myself; I have had one helluva time taking my eyes off of you in the car, and resisting my urges to hold you and smother you with kisses."

"If you had done that and someone saw it, we would both have been fired; now I'm hoping that this, from your point of view, isn't all just a strong sexual desire." Beth stated. "I haven't been as active in that area as I would have liked to have been, and my body has its needs, but I feel other things too, about you, Bob, beyond that basic desire. I know you to be a good man, a strong man, one who does not flaunt his own masculinity for the sole purpose of satisfying his sexual needs. Sex is a wonderful thing, but for a lasting relationship, which I hope this will be, I have always believed that couples must have a lot more in common. That trait wasn't there with the man I was married to, which I found out too late, but I do think that you and I have something more going for us, Bob; our working together for these past three or four months has made me realize just how compatible we are. I'm hoping that we are able to find that we have great compatibility in other areas . . . not just such as what I am thinking about right now. Why am I talking so much?!"

Bob pulled her over closer to him as he set his drink down on the coffee table, and Beth put her wine down as well. He put his hand behind her head and pulled it towards his mouth, and Beth responded by closing her eyes, pursing her lips, and moving her arms around him. Their kiss was long, wet, and lingering, until Beth pulled away a bit, saying, "I need to breathe! I haven't been kissed like that for a long time; in fact I have never been kissed like that! Whew!" She was almost gasping, shivering, and her body language was such that her desire for something more was growing; the excitement of the two was like a train gathering speed, and nothing was going to stop it or slow it down, nor did they want it to. Both of them began caressing each other, here and there, until the agitation grew beyond a stopping point. They moved almost silently toward the one bedroom, removing clothing as they proceeded, dropping pieces of clothing wherever they were removed, kissing each other as they awkwardly almost stumbled to the bedroom. They were nearly naked by the time they reached the bed, which they fell into in a full embrace. No words were necessary as they employed their hands and fingers to explore each other's body. Bob had grabbed his condom package from his jacket as they left the sofa, and he fumbled a bit, but was prepared by the time they were to join together, almost is a panic. It was ecstasy for both of them, and ended with such satisfaction that they were left completely exhausted. They slept peacefully, still entwined, and dreaming of each other.

TWENTY THREE

Over several days, Nurse Anne Whitcomb had accumulated all of the records that she believed attorney Justin Douglas said he wanted, plus a few others that she thought he would require. She also found a copy of the lease that covered the rental of the clinic's space in the office complex. When she thought she was prepared to meet with Douglas, which she was very reluctant to do, she called his office and left the message that she was prepared to meet with him when he was available, even if it were necessary to do so in the evening. He was not in at the time, but she soon got a call back from his secretary and was informed that he would be at the clinic within the hour. He was true to his word and arrived in forty-five minutes, entering the clinic in his usual blustery, impersonal manner, without any personal greeting, and giving the impression that he was in a hurry.

"My secretary said that you told her that you have gathered all of the records that I requested. Is that correct?" he asked.

"Well, I hope so," Anne responded, "Unless you have thought of something beyond what you had on your list. I did also find a copy of the lease for this office, and it is in that cardboard box (she pointed out), with all of the other papers. I have reconciled the two bank statements for the business accounts, but I did not open the one statement which I know is for a personal account of the doctor.

I also grouped all of the unpaid bills; they are in a large envelope in the box, all in alphabetical order. In the past, I normally wrote out all of the checks and Dr. Carnes would sign them before he left for the day. You and I had not talked about the procedure for getting the bills paid when you were here before, but I thought that perhaps you might prefer to write the checks yourself, or have your secretary do it. I never found it necessary to write the checks out more than once a week because there were never that many that needed to paid at any one time."

"That's fine, that's fine," Douglas said impatiently. "I'll just brief through this box and double check to see if everything I want is here. As long as the checkbooks are here, my girl can write out the checks for the bills when she has time. If any vendors call about bills that are due to be paid, just explain the situation to them and inform them that checks will be mailed out within the next day or so."

"I have already answered a few calls along that line, and will continue to do so, Mr. Douglas, but what about the mail; we will still be getting checks, advertising, inquiries about the practice, the usual stuff. Do you want me to just hold all of it for you, or would you want me to sort it, respond to any of it, or what?"

"Just let it pile up, Miss Whitcomb," Douglas answered tersely, "and I'll come by every day for awhile and pick it up, or have my secretary do it. Obviously, if you see something that is very important or urgent, I would expect you to call me immediately."

Nurse Anne said, "I don't want to interrupt what you are doing Mr. Douglas, but as I said before, this job is my principal income so I am naturally curious about whether you have found some other dermatologist to take over the clinic or just close it. I have been hoping that if you were to have found a buyer, the new owner would keep me on because I know the patients, the bookkeeping, and the files. Is there any chance that could happen?" Anne concluded.

Attorney Douglas looked annoyed, "I don't have time to get into that subject right now, Miss Whitcomb, I'm sorry," he replied, without showing any signs of regret. "As a matter of fact, if I am unable to locate a buyer, or potential buyer, by the end of next week, on Friday, you may consider it to be your last day of employment. I will see to it that you are paid up to date on that day. Should there be any change in what I have just explained, I will notify you. Do you understand?" he asked brusquely, in a manner that was unlike a real question. "The only exception to what I have just said is dependent upon the police investigation of the murder of Dr. Carnes. If they require the premises be open for any examination of records or whatever, then your presence will of course be necessary."

Anne was obviously disappointed with Mr. Douglas' statements, but she would not show how she felt, and merely affirmed that she understood. "Of course I will follow your instructions," was all she could utter. The lawyer took his box of records and left without expressing any degree of empathy for Nurse Anne's predicament, or any further adieu.

Nurse Anne Whitcomb sat there for awhile, pondering her future, and decided to call Mrs. Carnes in spite of Douglas' previous advice that it was not necessary. It was obvious that he did not want her to contact the widow woman for one reason or another. The nurse was glad that Opal Carnes answered the phone on the first ring.

"Opal Carnes," she answered the call, without hesitation or any show of emotion. That response surprised Anne because in the past, when she did answer the phone herself, it was always "Mrs. Carnes." To Anne it came across as reflecting a speedy mourning period, if there had really been one.

"Hi Opal, it's Anne Whitcomb."

"How are you, Anne; nice to hear from you; is everything alright?" Mrs. Carnes asked.

"Yes, I'm fine, Opal, other than having a disruptive meeting with Mr. Douglas; which brings me to the point of why I have called. You may know that Mr. Douglas had advised me not to bother you, but I felt that I should inform you as to what is happening here. Mr. Douglas just left with a box full of the records that he had asked me to assemble for him, and he informed me that a week from Friday could be my last day, unless he is able to find a buyer for the clinic. I was hoping to stay on here in the same capacity under a new owner, but I've gotten the feeling that Mr. Douglas doesn't care whether the clinic closes or not, or what happens to me. I hope you don't believe that I am off base by calling you, but I am curious as to whether you know anything at all about the situation here at the clinic."

Mrs. Carnes hesitated, seemingly not knowing exactly what to say. "I . . . I'm sorry Anne, there have been so many other things to take care of here at home; I have to confess I am in the dark about the clinic, but I don't mind your calling me at all, in fact, I appreciate your doing so. We have had Justin Douglas handle so much for us for such a long time that I may have relied on him too much since Richard died, but I have had little choice because I know so little about the business of the clinic. It may have been a mistake for Richard not to bring me into some of the affairs of the clinic while he was alive, but it's too late to think about that now."

'I don't want to trouble you over my dilemma, Opal, you have enough of your own concerns, so don't worry about me. One thing though, that does bother me," Anne went on, "is that I know that there is a large deposit being held by the building management company as security against the possibility of property damage being done if these premises were ever vacated, which was required under the terms of the lease at the time it was executed. I believe that it is fully refundable at the end of the lease period, or reduced after so many years of occupancy, depending on the condition of the premises at that time. I don't know exactly how much that would be at this point, but I wanted to make sure you knew about it. Please don't say anything to Mr. Douglas, but I have never felt like he had the degree of integrity that I felt lawyers should have. One last thing, would you please talk to him about providing some kind of severance pay for me? I worked for Dr. Carnes for a long time, as you know, and I feel that some severance pay, particularly under the circumstances, would be justified. Dr. Carnes also usually gave me a bonus at the end of the year, which I am sure I will not be getting this year, so I certainly could use some kind of severance pay, especially if I am going to be out of a job by a week from Friday. I can't tell you how much I would appreciate it."

"I understand, Anne," Mrs. Carnes replied, "and you shall have it; I will see to that, personally. Please let me know if Mr. Douglas does not take care of it, when and if you do have to leave."

Anne acknowledged the commitment and said, "Thank you very much, Opal. And please call me if I can do anything for you in return. I would be glad to come over and help you if you should need some assistance if you do decide to move. "They then ended their conversation. Anne was pleased with the response by Mrs. Carnes to the statements she had made; it all came off much better than what she had expected. She sat at her station for quite awhile, mulling over what her next move might be; she finally decided to call Detective Beth Reed. Reed was in her office and answered the call herself.

"Detective Reed here." She answered.

"It's Nurse Whitcomb," Anne announced. "I'm sorry to bother you, detective, and I don't want to waste your time, but I am a little upset with Dr. Carnes' lawyer, Mr. Justin Douglas. I may be on the wrong track here, and if so, don't hesitate to tell me so. He has made me believe that there is a good reason for why I am calling you; his conduct just strikes me as being less than the professional manner I would expect from a lawyer. Perhaps I'm overly suspicious, but it just doesn't seem that he is being completely honest with me."

"Don't worry about my time, Anne; we don't want to overlook any possible lead that may help to solve the doctor's murder. What is it specifically that is giving you such concern about Mr. Douglas' conduct?" Reed asked.

Anne said, "I don't know if I mentioned it before or not, but Mr. Douglas has taken complete control of the affairs here at the clinic and cautioned me, rather emphatically, not to bother Mrs. Carnes. He may have the perfect right to do so, but I can't believe he would not expect me to be talking to her after all of the years that I worked so closely with Dr. Carnes. Even though we have never socialized in a personal way, we have been on a first-name basis for years. Why would he do that? He had me gather all of the records, including the open check books, bank statements, and practically everything else, and he just left with a box loaded with everything related to the finances of the clinic. Maybe it's all okay, but I did talk to Mrs. Carnes, disregarding Mr. Douglas' directive, and she doesn't seem to know what's happening, and she seemed to be comfortable with my talking to her about Mr. Douglas. I know you have your investigation going on with those other people that were previously patients of the doctor, but it strikes me that maybe you should consider adding Mr. Douglas to your list. Maybe I'm being a little prejudiced, but the man just rubs me the wrong way. During the time that he has been with me, he has shown absolutely no remorse over the death of Dr. Carnes. What really ticks me off is that I'm not accustomed to being treated rudely; Dr. Carnes always treated me with respect. It also seems to me that one way or another, Mr. Douglas is in a position to take advantage of Mrs. Carnes, and she is very vulnerable right now, don't you think?"

Detective Reed accepted Anne's comments at face value, and replied, "I think that you are in a pretty good position to give a fair evaluation of the man, Anne, and please don't worry whether or not your comments are proper or not; we can't set limits on what anyone says during a murder investigation. I have no idea why he would want you not to talk to Mrs. Carnes; I agree with you that his conduct is not what I would expect, either, from a lawyer. Logically, It is very possible that Mr. Douglas may have much to gain from the assets of the clinic, with that in mind, we cannot rule him out as being involved with the death of the doctor, directly or indirectly. However, there is no question that we will do some checking on our lawyer friend, and it may be that we will have to confer with you again, Anne. In any event, we appreciate your call; it was the right thing to do." They each said goodbye and hung up. "Bob is going to let out a sigh when I tell him that we possibly have another suspect to investigate," she muttered to herself. "But that's our job," she said aloud.

TWENTY FOUR

Detective Beth Reed could see from her desk that her partner, Bob Garcia, was not on the phone, so she called him on the intercom and asked him, without any explanation, to come to her station. He put aside the documents he had been perusing and briskly walked the twenty feet or so to Reed's area; a quizzical look on his face. "You must have had something new pop up partner; good news, I hope?" he asked.

"Well oddly enough, Bob," Reed responded, "I had just been thinking that we should have had some contact with Dr. Carnes' lawyer, and out of the blue sky I get a phone call from Nurse Whitcomb. She is apparently quite unhappy with the attorney, a Justin Douglas, who she says has taken all of the financial records from the clinic without any discussion or any explanation to her or to Mrs. Carnes. Whitcomb also said he had previously instructed her to not bother Mrs. Carnes. In other words he does not want her talking to the widow lady; I don't see why he should have given her that instruction, unless he is doing something that is criminal or unethical. Nurse Whitcomb may be having a sour-grapes' beef because she expects to be out of a job by the end of the week, and Douglas has indicated he couldn't care less. However, we may find that her evaluation of the man is justified. He apparently has shown no remorse over the death of Dr. Carnes, and he has no interest in how the doctor's death affects Anne's life. Not the most sympathetic character, I guess."

Garcia picked up on the implication; "That sounds as though we are going to add Mr. Douglas to our list of possible suspects and put him through the grinder like the rest of our principals involved; correct?"

"Exactly," Reed confirmed. "I think that we are obligated to do so, Bob. Personally, I can't visualize a prosperous attorney stabbing anyone to death, but stranger things have happened. We also can't ignore the fact that he appears to be in a position to benefit financially from his administration of the clinic's affairs, or the disposition of its assets, that is if he is unable to find a buyer for the business. He is exercising full control, likely having obtained the legal right to do so, but with no one overseeing what he does. Nurse Whitcomb has said that since Mr. Douglas has free rein to do whatever he wishes, she is obligated to follow his instructions, at least for the moment. Let's hold off though, on getting a blood or saliva sample to establish a DNA profile for him. Nurse Anne could be way off base; we don't know her well enough to determine if there is any other reason for her resentment against the man. If we do get any information about his handling of the clinics' affairs in a dishonest manner, we can put the fraud guys on the follow up."

"Well if we are putting the lawyer aside right now, then should we start zeroing in on our Irishman, Sean McCoy, or what?" Garcia asked his partner. "I thought that we should review the Lab blood and DNA reports before we do anything else, Beth, unless you have some other idea. Another thing, I would think that the Lab would have prepared separate reports on the clothing examinations, if they have finished with that project. Time-wise, I think it's possible those reports could be on our desks this afternoon. Maybe they will provide us with information that will help us decide on our next step."

"You could be right, Bob," Beth Reed responded, "the sooner the better. In the meantime, we have Zach Segal in jail, so we don't have to worry about him right now. I called Roland LeBland's office early this morning and talked to his secretary. She informed me that he is in a hospital in Canada with a ruptured appendix. His secretary told me that he was in Toronto on business when he collapsed with pain; they are not sure when he will return to Florida, but they were assured by the hospital that he should be able to travel within a few days, depending on how well he responds to their treatment. With those two out of the way, at least temporarily, then we better pursue McCoy, but we should check on that Lab work first, before we do anything else. You call about that work and I'll see if I can set something up with the Jacksonville police department; I'm going to ask them to arrange to have Mr. McCoy meet us there, and to provide a conference room for us to conduct the interrogation. I'll have to check with the chief first to get his okay for us to drive to Jacksonville," and then she said quietly, with a wink and a smile, "Maybe we'll be forced to spend the night there."

Garcia grinned at his partner and said, "I wouldn't object to that; besides, I think that Hobson is leaning toward McCoy as the guilty party, basically because of the hat/cap connection. On the other hand I believe that you and I are on the fence with his thinking; we have both wondered what his motive might be; he surely had no personal gripe with Dr. Carnes. With Segal and LeBland it was obvious that both were angry because of financial losses that they blamed on Dr. Carnes, but why would McCoy murder the doctor? I'm sure that he never met the man, and he is only a half-brother, so I can't see that he would have such deep love for Marly that he would do it to satisfy her anger. Am I off the track here?"

"Not at all, Bob," his partner responded, "As you suspected, I feel the same way; yet we cannot ignore the cap thing. That is the only clue that we have that ties in with the killer, and we don't know whether there may be another motive by McCoy that hasn't been revealed thus far. Since we know he does not have the best reputation, and if he has been having a difficult time earning a living since he arrived here, money could be the motivation. Marly Brooks is a bitter person, and even though we believe, rightly or wrongly, that she has limited income, she just might have come up somehow with enough cash as an inducement to McCoy to do the deed for her. I think that if we are able to spend a little time with him, we might establish what the real relationship is between him and Marly. It might be a far closer relationship than the one that she proclaimed; they may even have been intimate back in Ireland when they were young. You go pester the Lab folks, Bob, and I'll talk to Hobson and then try to set up something in Jacksonville if the chief gives us the okay. I'll give you a ring or catch up with you at your desk when I'm through."

Garcia acknowledged his partner's plan, "That's fine, Beth; I'll get right on it, but if we do go and Hobson okays the overnight, we will have to leave in an hour or so. That would give us almost a full day there tomorrow, and then we could be back here by late afternoon. Otherwise we will have to leave from here fairly early tomorrow and just make a round trip of it. It wouldn't be nearly as interesting a trip as it would be if the chief approves the over-night plan." His dark brown eyes reflected brightly on the better possibility.

Reed nodded, a humorous glint in her own eyes, and said, "I know . . . believe me, I'll try for the overnight. I'm confident about his accepting the fact that McCoy has to be interrogated; the only hitch that I see might be that to conserve expenses, he may decide that only one of us needs to be there. As senior detective, he might feel I would be the one, but there's no guarantee on that point; he could just as well decide that you could conduct the interrogation on your own. On the other hand, I know he is a macho guy, and would hopefully want you to go with me as a matter of protection, if needed, and in the event of car trouble. I don't care what his thinking is, just as long as he gives us the okay." Garcia gave a wink to his partner, then left to return to his desk to make a call to the Lab and inquire about the status of the reports. Detective Reed crossed her fingers and then punched in the intercom number for the Chief of Detectives, Clyde Hobson.

TWENTY FIVE

Detective Reed played it very straight-faced with Chief Hobson when she requested the okay for her and Detective Garcia to drive to Jacksonville, explaining that to have most of tomorrow available to interrogate Sean McCoy, unless they were very lucky time wise, they would have to spend the night there. It was just too far, she reminded the chief, to drive back at night after the interrogation, which she indicated was likely going to be lengthy. She had previously called the Jacksonville Police Department and obtained the invitation to meet with McCoy at their office, adding that she would call their office again to confirm their meeting, after getting clearance for the trip from Chief Hobson. Hobson's demeanor gave no indication he thought of the trip as anything more than strictly business; to Reed it was clear he had no suspicions of anything going on between the two detectives because he did not hesitate to grant his approval of the trip. He was emphatic, however, when he said, "That's tonight only, Beth; unless something serious pops up, I expect you both back here by late afternoon to report the results of your questioning McCoy to me. Is that clear? And go easy on expenses . . . no caviar." But he was grinning when he said that.

"Of course, chief," Reed confirmed, while grinning in return. "The Jacksonville staff has been just great; they will have McCoy waiting for us at nine in the morning, and have even set up a special room for our interrogation. I have to call them back to confirm that Garcia and I will be there as planned, now that you have given us the okay. We're both hoping that this will wind up being the breakthrough on this case; from what we know, Clyde, McCoy seems to be a very likely person to have committed the crime. The one mysterious thing that we hope to resolve, is what could possibly be the man's motive." Using her partner's surname to add more credibility to the legitimacy of their trip together, she said, "Garcia and I have given some thoughts to that issue, and we expect to confirm the motive if our Irishman proves to be our man." Reed rose from the conference chair she had occupied, turned toward Hobson's office door, gave the chief a brief hand wave and said, "We'll see you tomorrow afternoon, chief, and we promise to stay within the budget." He nodded in agreement, and she left.

Detective Garcia looked up from reading the lab reports when he saw his partner approaching, a look of anticipation on his face. "Do I see a smile on that face?" he asked his partner.

"We got the okay, Bob, but we don't have any time to waste if we hope to be in Jacksonville before dark. And the chief was pretty strong about us being back tomorrow in time to give him a report on the interrogation." Reed then smiled and said, "And of course, we want to get there in time to enjoy the evening as much as we can."

"We will, we will," Garcia grinned back, "I'll see to that. I imagine you agree that we should have separate rooms, even though one of them might be wasted." He laughed, and Reed joined him in the thought.

"As a matter of fact, to further detract from anyone's suspicious thoughts in the office, if there are any, when I stopped by the reception desk I asked Cindy to book two rooms at the Motel Six there, and requested that they hold the rooms for late arrival. We may want to stop for dinner on the way, to save some time." Reed continued, "I also asked Cindy to call the Jacksonville Police Department and confirm our arrival there for the interrogation. I had called earlier to set it up with them, but had promised to confirm. That Cindy is a doll; she is always willing to do whatever needs to be done, and does it with a smile. You can drop me off at my apartment, Bob, so I can pack a bag; you run to your place and then come back as soon as you can. I shouldn't be long, maybe forty-five minutes."

Detective Garcia drove to Beth Reed's apartment, dropped her off as planned, then drove to his own apartment, washed up a bit, packed a small bag with what he felt would be needed, and returned to Beth's apartment in less than an hour. She was waiting for him outside of the building's door, her bag at her feet. As Garcia pulled up in front, Reed picked up her bag and was halfway to the auto before Garcia could open the door.

"Right on time, Bob; that's great," Reed greeted him. "We should make it to Jacksonville easily before dark now." She settled into the passenger's side of the front seat and moved close to her partner. The feel of her body next to him and the faint aroma of the squirt of perfume she had given herself made Garcia think about how quickly and safely they could make the trip. He even wondered if he could wait that long. The trip actually became more relaxed because Detective Reed fell asleep on the shoulder of her partner, and didn't awake until they were on the outskirts of the city of Jacksonville. That did make the drive safer for both of them, because there was less distraction for Bob, and he could concentrate on the road.

As the setting sun profiled the buildings of Jacksonville, Garcia nudged Reed's head a bit with his right shoulder and said, "Hey sleepy head, guess what, we're almost there." Reed brightened up, rubbed her eyes and looked out of her window as Garcia asked, "Do you have the motel's address, Beth? I think that you mentioned Harvey Lane, or something like that."

"Yes, here it is, 1313 N. Harvey Lane," Beth answered, looking at her notes. "As a matter of fact, I think that it should be right there," she pointed. "Off to the left, Bob, straight ahead; see the big sign? Just off of the corner on this street." Garcia saw the sign and turned at the next corner, right into the check-in covered driveway.

The team registered separately at the motel desk, agreed to meet at the motel dining room for a quick meal, and then found their way to their individual rooms. In less than ten minutes later they were seated in the dining room. Bob apologized for not stopping somewhere for dinner on the way. "I couldn't bring myself to waking you, Beth, you looked so relaxed; besides that I wasn't all that hungry myself. I munched on some trail mix I had in the console unit."

"As the young people say today, no problem, Bob; we will probably enjoy our meal here much more anyway, and we won't have to get right up from the table and go back to the car; now we can go to our rooms instead," she smiled. You order the drinks, Bob, while I look over this menu." The dining room was quiet, and the drinks that Bob ordered were delivered promptly, and the pair gave their dinner selections to the waiter.

Garcia lifted his glass of scotch as soon as it was served, and said, "To us, Beth, and to tonight, a night that I'm hopeful we will both long remember." They clinked glasses, smiled at each other in a loving way, with anticipation shining in their eyes. Bob's left hand held Beth's right hand while each just sipped their drinks. He said, "I guess we have to eat, but looking at you, Beth, it's hard to think about food." Fortunately, their simple light menu selections arrived before they had half finished their drinks, and they were soon able to adjourn themselves to their rooms, having left half of their dinners on their plates. As they were leaving the table, Detective Garcia said, in a humorous way, "I'll join you in your room so that we can discuss the murder case."

Beth laughed and said, "Of course partner, I'll be ready for some heavy discussion in a very few minutes." Detective Reed signed the dinner bill and they left for their own rooms.

"I didn't want to waste time knocking," Garcia said as he strode into Beth's room through the unlocked door not more than fifteen minutes later, without shoes or socks and with his shirt hanging outside of his pants. Their rooms were across the hall from each other, and the corner location provided them with considerable privacy. Beth Reed rose from the sofa she had been sitting in and walked to her partner, wrapping herself around him. They kissed passionately, not saying a word, moving their hands over each other's body, slowly loosening buttons and undoing hooks. They gradually moved to the king-sized bed, which was not very far away. By the time they reached the bed, which Beth had uncovered, they were half undressed. They eased their bodies unto the bed, where they completed the removal of their clothes, setting a record for clothing removal time, but they then relaxed, both seemingly wanting to extend the time of their enjoyment.

Garcia enjoyed the pace of their love making, caressing Beth's body where he knew she enjoyed it the most, while he held his own emotions in check. Eventually he had to succumb to his own desires, and he took the initiative to join their bodies. Although it seemed that it had taken them a long time to reach a climax, it was achieved simultaneously, and much more rapidly than they each expected. Nevertheless, they felt wonderful, and they knew more truly now than ever, that they would have a future together. They were now honestly bonded in love. Beth said it all when she expressed her feelings, almost whispering in his ear. "Now, Bob, I think that we are truly partners."

Bob Garcia added, "And I have to say, Beth, something I had not said to you before, although I have been thinking it for quite awhile. I now know for sure, that I love you." He was on his side, turned toward Beth, while she was prone on her back. He leaned on his right elbow as he stared at his partner, admiring her body, her long hair, and her half-closed eyes, then he slowly reached down and brought up the sheet to cover their bodies. He quietly nestled his head next to hers, and they quickly fell into a deep, peaceful sleep, each with a half-smile, contented look on their face.

TWENTY SIX

They both awoke early the next morning and did not wait until they had washed or scrubbed their teeth before embracing each other in almost a quiet manner, enjoying the passion of two people who have found great pleasure in their partner's mind and body. It was not necessary to talk much, but each was able to eventually express their love for the other. They fell asleep again, but just for a few minutes before Reed awoke with a start, and said, "I think that we better get a move on, lover, if we want to have any breakfast before we go to the meeting with our Mr. McCoy. I don't know about you, Bob, but I have somehow worked up an appetite."

Garcia laughed joyously and said, "Couldn't we just call in sick? Or maybe it would sound more reasonable if we reported that we had car trouble; I could slip out to the car and pull out a few wires. I've always been anxious to get moving in the morning and start working on some case or other, but not this morning."

"I wish we could prolong our stay here," his partner answered, "but that would for sure quickly raise some suspicions in Hobson's mind. That's the penalty for working for a boss that is also a detective; I worry about what might happen if and when he does realize that we are more than just a detective team. Anyway, do you mind if I take a quick shower?" She then laughingly added, "And even though it might be a lot of fun, I don't think that we have time for you to join me."

"No, you go right ahead . . . sweetheart; we'll have to do that some other time. I'll skip back to my room, shave, and take a quickie shower myself. Ring my room after you have finished your shower, and get dressed. I'll go down to the lobby and grab one of their little tables, where we can just have juice, coffee, and one of their advertised continental breakfast items. You come down when you're ready. We might be delayed for too long if we go into the dining room. I thought that we would we just leave after we eat; there is no way that we could go back to our rooms; not enough time. There is no question that we would get involved and be late for our meeting," Bob grinned at Beth.

She smiled, gave her partner a quick kiss and dashed to the bathroom; Bob left for his own room, and the couple then busied themselves with getting their morning ablutions completed, getting dressed, and gathering their things so that they would not have to return to their rooms. Garcia had arranged for an automatic check-out for both rooms when they had registered on arrival. Breakfast went quickly, both being satisfied with just one cup of coffee with their orange juice and sweet roll, after which they left directly for the Jacksonville Police Department's headquarters, which was only three blocks from the Motel Six. It was a brisk morning, but clear, so they decided that they needed the exercise and they walked the three short blocks. They felt invigorated by the time they got to the police building.

They were barely inside the front doors when a portly officer greeted them in a serious but friendly manner. "Good morning, I'm Officer Andrew Nichols, and I suspect you two are Reed and Garcia." He extended his hand to Detective Garcia and said, "I'd guess that you're Garcia."

Bob Garcia laughed and shook Nichols' hand and replied, "You've got that right, and this is Senior Detective Beth Reed," he said as he turned to his partner, who also gave Nichols her hand.

Reed then asked, "Is Sean McCoy here yet Officer Nichols? If he is, we would like to get started on the interrogation as soon as possible, because we have to get back to Orange Grove by mid afternoon, at the latest."

"I understand your time problem," Nichols stated, "but I think that you will not have to worry about that. We made sure that he got here early this morning because we wanted to check his identity and get him settled with some coffee in the main conference room before you arrived, which we did. He may be a little grumpy because of having to be here so early." Officer Nichols directed them by hand toward the conference room. "Just follow me around the corner. There is a pot of coffee there, cups, and whatever you need to go with it. Just help yourselves." The officer led them into the conference room, introduced them to McCoy and said, "Well he's in your hands; if you need anything just push that button at the left side of the table; I'll be available." Detective Reed thanked Nichols and he then left them with Sean McCoy, who hadn't said a word. He sat in a comfortable armchair, legs stretched out, and only nodded during the introductions. His facial expression showed no sign of emotion, and looked as though he was bored with the whole procedure. He was a fairly nice looking man, had a thick head of black hair, and was dressed in a gray sweatshirt, lightweight running togs, and gym shoes. He had more of an appearance of an athlete, rather than a killer . . . but then, who knows? Reed thought that the man may have dressed like the All-American boy in order to intentionally project a good-guy image.

Reed opened the questioning with saying, "We're not sure if you know why we had you brought in for questioning, Mr. McCoy, so I'll start off by confirming that you are what we call a party of interest in the case we are working on, that of the murder of a Dr. Richard Carnes. Has that information been given to you?"

McCoy was a slightly built man, about five-ten and a hundred and forty pounds. He had risen during the introductions, but now fidgeted a bit as he sat back down in the chair that he had been occupying; otherwise he did not seem to be disturbed by having been brought in for questioning, and did not hesitate to answer Reed's question. "All I know," he started, "is that I'm here because I am a half-brother to Marly Brooks and that the doctor that screwed her up was murdered.

To answer your question, I didn't know about the murder until Officer Nichols informed me about it an hour ago. I don't see how in hell you could think that I had anything to do with that." He replied with more than a bit of anger.

Detective Garcia made an effort to calm the man down, saying, "Mr. McCoy, right now all that we are trying to do is determine whether you might be connected in some way or another to the murder, and if we can determine you are not, then we can clear you from our list of people that we must evaluate as suspects. There have been no determinations made about you at this point; that's why we're here."

"You have confirmed your relationship with Miss Brooks, so that is one question now out of the way." Detective Reed stated, "Now we need to have you tell us two other things: How often have you visited her, and what were you doing on the early Saturday evening of September twenty-first, which I'm sure you have been told, was the time when Dr. Carnes was murdered?"

McCoy hesitated in answering, choosing to first sip some of his coffee, pausing as though he was contemplating how to answer the questions, but then replied to the first question. "As I'm sure you know, or can tell from my Irish accent, I have not been in this country very long, came over by steerage boat about six months ago. I wasn't able to locate Marly until two months ago, that's when I finally saw what happened to her. She had written to the family over there about the tragedy, but we really didn't fully realize how bad off she is. That bastard should have been stoned to death. Marly and I were pretty close when we were tots back home, and it riled my guts to see her; not the lively, healthy young lass she used to be. I haven't had much luck in making money over here, so I haven't been able to get down to see her very often, maybe every fortnight or so." He stopped talking and drank more of his coffee.

Detective Garcia then asked, "When you did visit her, did you stay overnight? And if you did, did you stay at her home, or did you go to a motel?"

"No," McCoy answered briskly, "I never went to a motel, couldn't afford it. I did stay with her one night when I thought it was too late to start driving back home. I was afraid the junker I own might not make it back to Georgia. I'm not sure when that was; seems to me it was a Friday night. I can't recall for sure about that particular Saturday night, the twenty first, you said. I've met a couple of guys while playing snooker, and we've started having a two-dollar game most Saturday nights; they're all singles, like me. Not much else you can do when your cash is low. Anyway, if it was a Saturday night I imagine I was playing pool that night."

Reed asked, "Do you think one of your friends might recall if you were with them playing pool on the night of the murder? If one of them could verify your presence on that night it would help to clear you. You and they should be aware of the possibility that they may be required to confirm their statement in court, depending on various factors. We can't establish that point as of right now; it will depend on whether one or more of your friends will step forward and confirm your presence at the pool hall on the twenty first."

McCoy looked concerned, he said, "I don't know about that; we likely had a few beers, as we usually do when we're playing pool or snooker, but one of them might remember my being there that night, or maybe the manager of place would remember me; I've never seen him drinking while he's busy managing the place; he would be more apt to recall who was there that Saturday, but I'll ask all of them about that night. But what are the other factors you're talking about?"

Garcia replied, saying, "We can't reveal that information at the moment, Sean, or answer any other questions you have; however, we would like to know if you normally wear a hat or cap, and if so, what kind?"

"Yes, I wear a green tam," McCoy said tartly, "What would you expect? I have two or three of them, all different shades of green, and I have a plaid one, but I don't wear one except at night; my thick black hair keeps me warm enough through the day. Why for God's sake would you want to know about my cap?"

"Again, Sean, we can't answer some of your questions at this time because this is an on-going investigation." Reed replied, "Of course when the case is finished we might satisfy your curiosity, all of which depends on whether you become more, or less than a party of interest to us. We have your blood or saliva samples, as you know, and our Lab has by now determined your DNA, so our next step is to decide where we are going with you. In the meantime, I suggest that you contact your pool playing friends as soon as possible, and see if you can come up with a witness to your presence at the pool hall on the evening of September 21st. You can reach us at the number on the card I handed you when we were introduced, so you can call us if you are able to find someone. I am not going to ask for your passport at this point, but I am cautioning you to not leave the country. That would jeopardize your future here, and by doing so it would be interpreted as an indication that you were guilty of something to do with the murder of Dr. Carnes."

"We have no objections to your talking to your sister about this questioning session," Detective Garcia stated. "However, you should be conscious of the possibility that somewhere down the road you may be in need of a lawyer; it is too early to make that determination. Not just because you might need to be defended in this case, but you might need one if you wish to stay in this country. The immigration department may ask that your Visa permit be canceled if they are convinced that you were involved in Dr. Carnes' murder, even if no charges have been filed against you. We will not be notifying them of your possible involvement at this time, but we will be required to do so if we obtain confirmation that you are involved. We are also asking you to inform us immediately if you should move to another residence."

Sean McCoy paled and his face reflected a combination of anguish and anger, but he restrained himself, giving vent only to his inner emotions. "Well that's a helluva nice welcome to the good old USA. First my sister suffers irreparable physical damage from an inept dermatologist, and now, after only six months in this country, I become a suspect in the murder of a man I never knew. Quite a welcome!' he almost shouted.

Senior Detective Reed rose to leave, and her partner did likewise, "We're sorry, Mr. McCoy, you have to understand that we are only doing our job. We're leaving now; I'll tell Officer Nichols that we are leaving and that you are free to return to Georgia. We thank you for your time." The team shook the limp hand of Sean McCoy and left.

As they walked down the hallway to the lobby and the exit door, Bob Garcia said to his partner, "What do you think, Beth? Is he an actor, a good liar, or what? He seems sincere, but yet he has that bit of Irish flair about him that doesn't quite ring true. In spite of the time we have spent with him, he is still an enigma in my mind. Or maybe I've got a bit of jealousy in me about that enchanting Irish brogue."

"Hey there, my good man," Beth said with a laugh. "Did you forget that Reed is an Irish name? All kidding aside, Bob, I understand what you're saying. We didn't get into the subject, but I would like to know more about his personal life. He's a nice looking young man, but he said nothing about any love life, nor did he indicate how he is making a living. I noticed that he was dressed very casually, but clean, and his hands did not appear to have had much to do with manual labor. No dirty fingernails; maybe he's a gambler. Anyway, I had those questions in the back of my mind, as you may have had, but I thought if he does come up with an iron-clad alibi for that Saturday night, then any further questioning will be moot and we can chalk him off the list."

"Okay partner, then let's shove off for home." Garcia said. "If we can keep the meeting short with Hobson, we might still enjoy what's left of the day." Beth gave him a knowing smile as they climbed into their car. She had no sooner buckled her seat belt than she put her head on Garcia's shoulder and immediately fell asleep. He looked over at her and smiled happily.

Detective Bob Garcia cautioned himself about keeping his eyes on the road instead of admiring his partner, who quietly slumbered on his right shoulder. He was pleased that the traffic was light and that he could drive the return trip back to headquarters in Orange Grove at a leisurely pace. The interrogation of Sean McCoy had been accomplished in less time than the team had expected, so there was no concern about arriving in time for the meeting with Chief Hobson. With the McCoy session over with, and with the quietness of his partner, Garcia found himself reflecting on his life thus far, and how fate had provided him with a new life, one which began with becoming a police department team member with Beth Reed. He started to envision what his future life might be, and if it would be with Beth as his partner for life.

"How lucky can I be?" he asked himself. He mentally reviewed parts of his life that had most affected him, starting with thinking about how his parents had fled Cuba just a few months before he was born, and how later he was happy to realize that that move entitled him to declare he was a citizen of the United States of America; a fact that gave him great joy. He had always been grateful his parents had the intelligence, and the opportunity, to leave the restricted life they had led in that island country. He also thought back how legally, and illegally, several other family members were able to join his family in the states; and that almost all of them had eventually become true citizens of their new country. Most of them had settled in the little town of Homestead, south of Miami; some of them had decided to stay there. The climate was not unlike that of Cuba, which eased their adjustment to the new country. At the same time he sorrowed over; the fact he could not visit Cuba and renew relations with those few members of his family that remained. Too, the music he had learned to love was never heard in Orange Grove.

His muse continued as he drove to Orange Grove, unable not to glance over once in awhile to admire his partner, the woman he had come to love. He thought back to the time when they were first introduced, and his apprehension about becoming a subordinate to a woman. That feeling, he recalled, had quickly disappeared soon thereafter when her words and actions proved that she was very intelligent and was conscious of the natural competitiveness that might develop, and possibly even friction, were she not to have the temperance and personality that made the association workable. During the roughly three months they had been partnered, he could not recall a time when they had any personality problem.

His mind skipped back to the time when his father announced that they were going to move to Tampa from Homestead, where he had made a lot of friends playing soccer as a pre-teenager. As a barber, his father knew that he could make a better living in a larger city, not a high income, but a steady income, instead of the pay he made as a construction laborer. Detective Garcia's trauma faded, he remembered, because in high school he had been able to become a member of the R.O.T.C. That training in turn had led to his becoming a police-trainee, then a patrolman for eight years before becoming qualified and then elevated to the position of detective. He marveled, as he had many times, at what his life has been, and how his good fortune was possible because he was a U. S. citizen. He had little connection with anyone in Cuba anymore, and wondered about distant aunts, uncles, and cousins that were still in Cuba, and what their lives must be today.

Beth Reed stirred a bit and shifted her body, bringing Garcia out of his reminiscence. He suddenly became aware of the fact that they were almost back in Orange Grove. He moved his shoulder a little and his partner sat up, wide awake. "Oh, my gosh!" she said, "I can't believe that I've slept all the way back. Why didn't you wake me, Bob? I feel badly you didn't have any company for the drive back."

Bob Garcia laughed, "No problem, Beth. I enjoyed just looking over at you from time to time, and I was having a mental review of my life . . . thus far."

"And?" Reed questioned.

"It has been good," Garcia replied, "Much better than I ever thought it would be." He smiled, and looked quickly into Reed's hazel eyes. "And because of you, it is getting better all the time."

"May I say, detective Garcia," Reed said light heartedly, "That you have made this trip most enjoyable for me, and I hope it has also been enjoyable for you."

Garcia reached over and squeezed Beth Reed's hand, and said, "It was fantastic, Beth. We should try to see if we can arrange for more trips out of town." They both laughed at that thought.

They pulled into the parking lot at the police headquarters, as they both were forced into assuming their normal detective demeanor.

TWENTY SEVEN

The team arrived back at the Orange Grove Police Headquarters about four-fifteen and found Chief Detective Hobson awaiting them, somewhat impatiently; he immediately waved them to the two conference chairs in front of his desk. "I don't like having to rush this meeting guys," he said, "and I apologize for it, but I forgot all about the high school graduation of one of our four grandchildren set for early this evening, so if you don't mind let's get right to the crux of your interrogation of Mr. Sean McCoy."

"That's fine, Chief," Detective Reed assured him. "We've had a long day, and we're both ready for dinner; we skipped lunch to make sure we got back here as soon as we could. We will be as brief as possible, but I did want to say a word or two about the Jacksonville Police Department because we may need to work with them again sometime in the future. They had McCoy set up in a pleasant conference room, including fresh coffee when we got there. Officer Nichols introduced us all around to Sean McCoy, and then left us alone with the man; when we left we of course thanked him for the courtesies that had been extended to us. When we finished with the interrogation, we told him that it was alright to let McCoy leave. It was all very professional."

"I'm glad to hear that, Reed," Hobson replied, "Our units have worked with other Cities, but this is the first time that we have worked with Jacksonville. When you have a moment, please give me Officer Nichols' phone number; I would like to discuss a few administrative matters with him. His operation is a lot bigger than ours, and he may give us some ideas on how to improve our organization. It seems that more and more we have bring in members of other police departments in order to help us solve some cases, whether it is with Jacksonville, Miami, or whoever. I'm glad that you had a good experience there. Now tell me about this Sean McCoy; does it appear that he is to be taken as a serious suspect in the Carne's murder case, or did it turn out to be another blind alley?"

Reed answered the question with some hesitancy. "I wish that we could give you a positive answer on that chief, but there are still some unanswered questions about the man. As we expected, he made a forceful denial of any connection to the murder of Dr. Carnes; he said he had only just heard about it from Officer Nichols as he was brought in for questioning. On the other hand, he was a bit glib, and almost overreacting to our questions. I believe that there is definitely a question of credibility. To sum it up, Bob and I both view McCoy as a serious prospective guilty party, don't we, Bob?"

"If Beth didn't indicate that he is positively a candidate," Garcia responded, "it is because even though we agree that he is looks like number one right now, we have to confirm our suspicions about his statements. He is an innocuous appearing man, probably about five-nine or so, maybe one-fifty, and cagey. His facial expressions and body language were hard to read, particularly because of his heavy Irish accent. He is either a good liar or a good actor; we haven't made up our minds about that, but on the ride back we discussed the feasibility of having him take a lie detector test. I would expect him to refuse to have the test if he is really the killer. If he is, we will have to come up with some convincing evidence; and right now we have very little to be able to make that connection."

Reed took over the reporting again. "McCoy confirmed that he is the half-brother of Marly Brooks and made no bones about how very angry he is about what Dr. Carnes did to her. Apparently they were very close when they were teenagers back in Ireland. He has only been in the U.S. about six months, doesn't seem to have a steady income, but has visited Brooks a few times since he came over. The really encouraging thing that we learned in terms of connecting him to the murder is the fact that he owns and wears a tam when he goes out for the evening. In response to our questions, he revealed that he has three green colored tams, all being of various shades, and one plaid one. He didn't hesitate to tell us that when we asked him if he wore a hat, possibly because he knew we would find that out anyway, or he never thought about that being any kind of a clue in the murder. We did not, of course, tell him that the tam is a clue in this case. If he ultimately does take a lie-detector test, and he fails it, then we might want to have Mr. Sandvick, the clerk, view McCoy in a line-up wearing a tam. It is possible that he could make an identification, even if it is from some sort of profile. That would be a stretch, but stranger things do happen."

Garcia picked up on the reporting; "He said that he spends a lot of his Saturday nights playing pool or snooker with some regulars down at a local pool hall in Brunswick, but he could not say where he was the night of the murder. We suggested he try to get one of his pool buddies to confirm he was at the pool hall that night, or if any of them were with him at another location on that Saturday. If that falls through, which Beth and I think that it will, then he has no alibi for that night. We asked him to call us if a friend does step forward; he is also to ask the pool hall manager about confirming his presence the night of the murder, that is if he was really there at the time."

Hobson rubbed his chin as he rose from his chair and nervously paced back and forth behind the desk, while finger brushing his thick mustache. "I'll personally get on the phone with the Jacksonville Chief Detective and arrange for a lie detector test for McCoy. We need to get that out of the way before we go any further with Mr. McCoy. From what you have told me, I think that he is shaping up as the killer, but I previously said that I thought that the real connection would prove to be related to blood evidence. I still feel that way. Have you both gone over the lab reports in detail? You should have all of the various DNA numbers, but what about the tech's examination of the clothing of the others that are involved in the case, one way or another? Even though McCoy is our number one suspect at this moment, we can't stop investigating our other leads; you both know that that is our obligation."

"We're aware of that Clyde. We're not letting up on anyone at this point. If you agree, Chief, tomorrow morning we will review all of the lab reports that are available, and then we want to follow up on Mr. LeBland, who should be recovered enough from his appendectomy operation to be back in this country by now. We may even have time to talk to Zach Segal while he's in the slammer. We are still a long way from arresting anyone for the murder, so we can't ignore any of the others involved, including the Carnes lawyer, whom we have yet to question, but whose name we have added to the Lab list for blood and DNA analysis."

Hobson stopped pacing and assented to the team's work plan. "Go ahead with those ideas, and I'll let you know the results of the lie detector test for McCoy, that is if they will set it up and conduct it for us. Get back to me on the blood checks; I want to know if all of the clothes that were examined were found to be free of blood specks, or if any specks found were sufficiently large enough to provide the Lab with enough to conduct the analysis work. Sorry to cut this short, guys, but I have to leave now. Anyway, thanks for making it back in time to meet with me, and I'm glad that everything worked out well for you in Jacksonville." The two detectives showed no outward emotion with that comment, but internally they were thinking, "Oh yes, it could not have been better."

The two rose from their chairs, gave the Chief a wave, and left the room. Reed said to her partner as they walked toward the exit, "Bob, I think we have to try and eliminate one or two of our suspects, and zero in on the one or two of them we feel most strongly about. If we are able to identify Segal's accomplice, bring him in for questioning, then we may be in a position to either drop Segal from the list, or obtain enough new information to put him at the top of the list. I'm sure the killer is among the group that we are working on, but we seem to have gotten bogged down with this case. Remember, Hobson wanted us to interrogate Segal anyway, to see if we can get the name of his partner in the scam they were trying to execute. He may be reluctant to admit that, but if it helps to save his butt, one way or another, I think that he would loosen up. Let's meet at the jail tomorrow morning; I'll make the call and set it up. I'm anxious to remove someone from our list, and I have a feeling that it's going to be Mr. Segal. What do you think, Bob?"

Garcia nodded in agreement. "He looked like a prime suspect when we first got into this case, but now we have Mr. MCoy, and we still have LeBland to clear, not to mention Carnes' lawyer. So if our meeting goes quickly tomorrow morning, we could just pop in on Mr. LeBland, if he is available. I'll see you at the jail at nine in the morning, unless you call and tell me a different time. Okay?"

Reed nodded in agreement and said, "That will work out just fine, Bob. I have some shopping to do tonight and I have to call my brother, but could we plan for a dinner out this next weekend, or am I rushing things?"

"Not for me, Beth; I was hoping that we could enjoy the weekend together. I'll plan it and buzz you later as to where and when tomorrow," Garcia replied, giving Reed a broad smile, with a bright spot in his brown eyes.

TWENTY EIGHT

After showing their credentials to the security guard at the county jail, the pair of detectives were ushered through the double security gates into a small conference room, which held one small Formica covered table and three plain straight chairs. There was no room for anything else. An observation camera was mounted in a ceiling corner, directed in a position that would cover all three chairs. The prisoner, Zach Segal, was sitting in one of the chairs, head down, a glum look upon his face, which was unshaven, and his hair looked like it had not seen a comb in days. He looked up with bloodshot eyes as the detectives entered the room, which the guard locked behind them. Segal gave them a short sullen greeting: "Oh, it's you two; I wondered who my visitors were. Now what? Is this what you guys call the third degree?"

Segal's questions were ignored by both detectives. "How do you feel about possibly taking a lie-detector test, Mr. Segal?" Detective Reed asked, almost rhetorically, just to get a reaction.

"For Christ's sake! What for?" Segal questioned angrily, "I've already been put through the mill on the scam thing, and that's not such a big deal; it didn't work out anyway. Why should I have to have a lie detector test? There's nothing more to learn from that; I've already told you all I know about the murder of Dr. Carnes."

Reed answered him. "Calm down, Mr. Segal; we need to know more about that partner you had in trying to work your scam on Mrs. Gordon. We want you to tell us the name of that man and where we might find him. I would think that you would realize because of his connection with you, we must also consider him to be a party of interest in the murder of Dr. Carnes. We must clear him from our list of suspects as the possible killer, or confirm that he is innocent."

"Killer!" Segal almost shouted. "Why would he be a suspect in that murder? What would his motive be? I'm the one Carnes screwed, not Sam! Oh shit!" Segal swore at himself for letting his anger influence his objection to Reed's statement, and revealing his accomplice's first name.

"Thank you, Mr. Segal," Reed responded, "at least now we have his first name; now you might just as well give us his surname. We'll get it one way or another, and soon, I'm sure that you realize that. Giving us his last name is what we call cooperation, and in your position it would seem smart for you to cooperate." Reed and Garcia sat back and let her comments sink into Segal's brain, and make him realize it would be to his benefit to give them Sam's last name, but he sat there sullenly, mulling over what options he had, and deciding how he should reply.

Detective Garcia got up and grabbed Segal's shoulder, shaking him just a bit to awaken him from what almost looked like a stupor, and make him realize that it would be to his advantage to cooperate. "Don't you see," Garcia asked, "that we have to consider the possibility of your having paid him to get your revenge against the doctor? As we see it, you could have had some kind of trade-off with Sam, for one reason or another, so perhaps no money would have to be paid. We know that there are a lot of hired killers that do not come from the Mafia; there are others; maybe Sam is one of them. One way or another, we will find out."

Detective Reed again took over the questioning. "At this moment the fraud squad is working on evidence that we fully expect will reveal the last name of your partner in crime, but we want to have that name now. If we clear him, then you will probably also be removed from our list of suspects in the murder case; so you will only have to worry about the scam charge." Both detectives sat back and waited to see Segal's reaction to what Reed had said.

"If I give you that information," Segal inquired reluctantly, "will you then tell the prosecutor on the fraud case that I cooperated with you? I know that you can't make any promises about my getting leniency, but that usually does help, doesn't it . . . my cooperating?"

Garcia interjected his own answer, "Yes, Mr. Segal, it usually does help, but you have to understand that it will only be of benefit to you if the information you furnish is valid. We want the full name of your partner, as you know it, not just a nickname, and we need an address where he can be found. Do you understand?"

"Of course I understand," Segal confirmed, a bit huffy. "His name is Sam Meyers, spelled M-E-Y-E-R-S, and I only know him as Sam; his first name might be Samuel, I don't know. I haven't known him a long time; we got hooked up some time back when he would place bets for me with a local gambling syndicate. Unless he has moved, he has an apartment on twenty-second street; offhand I think it is 6344, apartment number 16. I'm sure you smart guys can find it." Zach Segal was breathing heavily. It was apparent that he was going to continue talking, but he first had to settle himself down. The detectives were concerned that he might not be able to continue; he looked like a man ready to have a stroke or a heart attack. He finally got himself together and said, "When we were working on the appraisals and pictures for the jewelry thing, I gave Sam a key to the antique shop, so it's possible that you might find him there. To make a few bucks I wouldn't be surprised at his keeping the door open and making some sales. If you catch up to him, he'll be ticked off at me for giving you his name, but he may feel a little better if you tell him that I will pay the bills for the defense attorney we will have to get. Otherwise he'd have to settle for one of those young inexperienced public defenders."

"Since you were such good buddies," Reed asked somewhat sarcastically, "Would it be possible that you would have known where Meyers was on the evening of September 21st? The night of the murder."

Segal's breathing seemed to have returned to somewhat normal, and he was able to answer without any difficulty. "Not hardly," he said. "If you remember, I told you about my activity that night . . . the motel thing and then boozing it up a little. I have no idea what Sam was doing that night. As far as I know, he's single, so he was probably out hunting up some action." Segal made an effort at making a knowing grin.

"Well I really expect that the fraud squad will find him before we do," Garcia stated. "He may be joining you in your cell before long." Detective Reed nodded in agreement, then concluded the meeting; leaving Mr. Segal sitting dejectedly in his chair. The team left the interrogation room, signaling the guard that Segal could be returned to his cell.

Bob Garcia turned to his partner as they left the jail, and asked her, "Well what do you think, Beth? He is a pathetic character, but is it too soon to scratch him from our list of suspects?"

"I think so, Bob; I wouldn't feel comfortable doing that right now, at least not until we clear Sam Meyers. If we are convinced that Meyers had nothing to do with the murder, then I think we can scratch Mr. Segal. I don't believe that either of us ever thought that Segal could have stabbed anybody, but perhaps Meyers would have been capable. We'll see."

"Unless you have something else in mind, Beth, do you think now would be a good time to pay a visit to our world traveler, Mr. LeBland?" Bob Garcia asked. "We have nothing scheduled for the afternoon, as far as I know."

"I know we discussed doing that, Bob, but on second thought, I think the most pressing thing for us to do is to review the lab reports. Hobson is probably right in that we will eventually find our killer through a blood connection. I suggest we go back to the office, sit down in a conference room and see if there is some clue in any of the lab reports that are finished. We might also get lucky and find the Jacksonville guys have completed the lie detector test of our immigrant Irishman. I think we both feel we have not been making the progress on this case that we should have by this time, and we are running out of suspects. We may have to sit back and take another look at everything we do have. We may have to take a totally different approach. Right now all that we are sure of is that the doctor was the victim of a premeditated murder, and we're very short of clues that could connect us to the killer, whoever that might be. So let's head to the office; if Hobson is there, maybe he will have a different slant on the info we do have, and a thought about what our direction should be."

Garcia recognized the truth of what his senior partner was saying, although he was not happy to hear it. "You're getting to read my mind, Beth, I agree, but only if we can stop at some fast food spot and you let me buy us lunch."

"I'm a bit hungry too, Bob, but as your superior," she laughed, "I insist on buying."

Garcia grinned at her offer, and said, "You know, Beth, I am smart enough not to argue with a superior. Let's go."

TWENTY NINE

Neither of them had called in before arriving at headquarters and were disappointed when they learned from the receptionist that Chief Detective Hobson was out on another case with other detectives. Cindy also told them that he had said that he did not expect to make it back to the office before the end of the day. Reed took the blame; "I don't know why I didn't think to have one of us phone in to see if the chief was going to be available; damn it . . . he could even have been out to lunch. Well partner, it's not like we don't have enough to do, so we certainly won't waste the time. We have both wondered about Miss Brooks' financial situation, and I think that we should examine her bank account at the Chase bank today, that is, if we can make the arrangements. Would you mind getting a Court Order for us to have the bank let us review her account for the last year or two? I'll call the bank and prepare them for our arrival so they can print out the account numbers beforehand, and save us some time. I'll also ask them if they could provide a private conference room where we can review and discuss the account records; I would hope that they will have some knowledgeable person available to answer any questions that I'm sure we will have; those computerized print outs are always confusing to me when I first start to read them."

"I'll get right on it, Beth," Garcia affirmed. "If there is any kind of a delay because they have to wait for someone to get a judge to sign it, I'll nevertheless see you as soon as I can back at our work stations. If you get things set up at the bank quickly, what would you think about calling LeBland's office and see if and when he might be available, just in case the bank can't accommodate us this afternoon. If I remember correctly, his office is not too far from the downtown Chase Bank building. Depending upon his availability, we could time the meeting with him either before or after we have our meeting with the bank folks."

"That's a good idea, Bob; I'll still probably finish with my calls before you get back, so you might just as well look for me at my desk. If you get the Court Order without any problems, we should be able to get to the bank before noon. Good luck in getting that order; see you soon, I hope. If I wind up working a time in for us with Mr. LeBland, I'll leave a note about it on your desk." With that settled, Detective Reed departed for her work station.

Detective Reed went to her work station and Garcia took the stairs, two at a time, up to the offices where a dozen law clerks were busy with papers. He was happy to find that one of the clerks was available to help him; he explained the situation, and gave the clerk the information needed to prepare the Court Order. "This won't take me long to prepare, detective, but I can't promise how quickly I can get a judge to sign it," the clerk said apologetically. "You'll have to sit over there in the lounge area and wait, unless you want to leave and then come back. As soon as I get it signed, I'll bring it to you, if you stay, otherwise, I'll give you a ring at your desk. There's a coffee station set-up there; help yourself."

Garcia thanked the clerk and walked over to the lounge area, poured himself some coffee and sat down to mentally review the facts of the Carnes' case. He felt frustrated by the realization that he and Beth had not been able to zero in on a path that would lead them to who murdered Dr. Carnes, nor could they even feel any confidence in concluding which of the several known suspects could actually be the killer. Both detectives had voiced the thought that the killer could very possibly be someone else, a person that is not on their current list of suspects. Garcia asked himself, "Who else could be involved? Have we missed learning about some other individuals who were connected to Dr. Carnes some way or another? Could there be an old, old enemy from college days, or a nutty family relative that no one likes to talk about? Who? Who else can there be?" He agonizingly questioned himself, and began to doubt his own ability as a detective, and found himself sympathizing with Beth Reed, who likely felt inadequate herself. "Damn!" he muttered to himself, "We need a break, and soon, or Hobson may be thinking of taking both of us off of the case and turning it over to another team."

He finished his self-admonition and his coffee at about the same time; he looked at his watch to check the time just as the law clerk entered the area with the order in his hand. "Well, detective," he said, "you are in luck; I was able to catch Judge Arnold a moment before he was to leave for lunch. Here is your Court Order. I hope that it gets you what you're looking for."

Garcia thanked the clerk, took the order from his hand, and made a bee-line for the stairs to take him down to meet with Reed. He waved the order toward her as he approached her desk; "Got it," he said cheerfully, coming out of his funk. "Are we set at the bank? Or are we heading to LeBland's office?"

"Yes, and no, Bob," Reed answered. "Everything has been arranged with the bank; they should have Marly Brooks' records for the last two years available when we get there, and they will have a private conference room for us to use. The 'no' is that we are not going to LeBland's office, at least not today. He has returned from Canada, but apparently is not physically up to going back to work just yet. That's okay with me; in my opinion he is not near the top of our list anyway. Let's head down to the bank; one of the banks' vice presidents, a John Goodwin, said either he or one of his assistants will help clarify any questions we may have. So you go get our chariot while I make a potty stop, and then you can pick me up at the front of the building. Okay?" Garcia grinned at her comment, nodded in agreement and left to get the car. By the time Bob Garcia had driven from the parking area to the front of the building, Detective Reed was there, waiting for him, and they left for the Chase Bank.

The bank's vice president, John Goodwin, rose from his desk when he saw the team enter the bank, knowing without being told that they were the detectives he had expected. After introductions, he led them to the conference room he had reserved, had an assistant bring in the printouts of the Brooks' account, and left them to do their examination, after pointing out a call button in the event that some clarification was needed. "Buzz if you need assistance," he said in departing.

As the team reviewed the debits and credits to the account it was obvious to them that there were no large amounts involved at anytime during the previous two years, and in total there was little financial activity. Brooks' Social Security check had been credited automatically every month, and some small bills were debited to the account through the bank's Sure-Pay system. One transaction that did stand out was a $400.00 amount that was credited to the account each and every month of two years being examined. "Hey! Where did that come from?" Garcia asked.

"That question also came to my mind quickly, after seeing that number pop up two months in a row, Bob, but I didn't expect to see it every month. Miss Marly hasn't said anything about those deposits; she may have some plausible reason for not doing so, I imagine; we'll see. Miss Brooks gives us one surprise after another. We need to know more about that money; we better get Mr. Goodwin, or someone, to come in here and help us find out the source of those deposits. I'm sure that their coding system will indicate whether or not the deposits were made in cash. We'll have to ask Mr. Goodwin, or an assistant to clarify that question for us. Push that call button, Bob; somebody will come in . . . soon, I hope."

A young lady opened the door to the room in just about one minute after Garcia pushed the button. "Mr. Goodwin is tied up at the moment, but I'm his assistant and he asked me to respond to your call. Could I help you?" she asked. "My name is Rebecca."

Detective Reed introduced herself and Detective Garcia to the young lady, and then explained what case they were working on. She then inquired about the regular cash deposits that had been made to Brooks' account for the last two years. The young lady proved to be of more help than they expected. "I probably know more about that account than anyone else," she offered, "I was a teller here for several years before I was promoted to being the assistant to Mr. Goodwin. Starting quite a few years ago, a man, who was probably middle-aged, started to come in around the middle of each month and made a cash deposit to that account; I waited on him many times. I think the records show they are still being made, and still in cash. I know who Miss Marly Brooks is, and of course everyone in the bank eventually learned about what happened to her; a real tragedy. She rarely comes into the bank. To my knowledge, no one in the bank has ever discussed those deposits with her. We have all been glad that someone seems to be helping her. The money may or may not come from the man making the deposits; we have no way of knowing; I don't believe anyone here knows his name. He was not very talkative, but he was always polite and said thank you when he received the deposit slip. I had often wondered if he could just be doing it for someone else who wants to remain anonymous. Can I help you with any other questions?"

Reed and Garcia looked at each other, both taken aback by this new revelation. Reed collected her thoughts and finally asked the young lady if she could describe the man that had been making the deposits. "Well I can tell you what he looked like when he first started to make the deposits, because I was a teller then, and he seemed to come to my window whenever he came in; I was usually at the first window away from the waiting line. He seemed to be pretty healthy to me at the time, but as I said, he didn't talk much. When he did talk, he was pleasant and quiet. He was slender, but not skinny; around five-ten, with sort of sandy hair. I have had a desk around the corner from the teller stations for a long while now, so I don't see him very often anymore, and then it is only at a glance. He always came in alone, so I don't know if he is married or not. I noticed that he always filled in the deposit slip from the supply in the waiting line area; I presume that he still does that. Is there anything else that I can help you with?"

Detective Reed replied to the woman's question, "You have been more helpful than we ever expected, Rebecca, and we thank you for your time. I believe that we are finished with our examination of the records now, so you can arrange to re-file all of these records, but please tell Mr. Goodwin that we may need to have them available in the event that they would wind up being required in court. Please also let him know that we appreciate the assistance he, you, and the bank have given us in the murder case we are attempting to solve." The young lady was gathering records together as the team left the conference room, a bit stunned to learn that the murder case of Dr. Richard Carnes, which she had read about, was the reason for the detectives to be there examining account records, particularly those of Miss Marly Brooks.

The partners kept silent until they were seated in their car. Garcia did not start it up; he sat there trying to determine what their examination of Brooks' banking records had revealed. Was it the key that would unlock the mystery of the murder of Dr. Carnes? What could a piddling $400 a month have anything to do with a murder? If their inquiry at the bank resulted in it having nothing at all to do with the murder of Dr. Carnes, would it be construed to have merely been snooping in a personal matter? Not the kind of thing that the department would want to have publicized. It all seemed too ridiculous to Bob Garcia. Reed too, sat silently for a moment, wondering if Sean McCoy had anything to do with the cash deposits, but she then quickly put that thought aside, realizing that he had only been in the country a short while, long after the deposits had started being made. Were drugs and drug money involved somewhere along the line? If thousands of dollars were involved, it would be more likely that some more profound criminal element would be evident; thus far it had not been.

Was there a connection with some relative in Ireland who wished to remain anonymous, someone who was providing the funds? The two detectives pondered over the possibilities. Reed broke the silence with a firm decision: "I don't see how we can do anything, Bob, other than face Marly Brooks with our question about the source of the cash deposits. She can't play games with us on that; she has to have known where the money came from. Whether it turns out to be a personal thing, and perhaps a little embarrassing for us, or not, we have to get the question answered. Forget Mr. LeBland for now, Bob, drive to Marly Brooks' place."

Garcia started up the car, a look of perplexity on his face, but he didn't hesitate to endorse his superior's decision. "I agree with you completely, Beth, but now I am wondering how we can learn the identity of the man who made the deposits. It may be that Marly Brooks really doesn't know the name of her benefactor, either that or she won't tell us, for some reason or another. She has definitely not been altogether forthright with us."

"You know that I am a positive person, partner, so I am not even entertaining that line of thought. I would think that by now Miss Brooks is probably so sick of us that she is likely ready to tell all just to get us off her back; at least I hope so. In any event, as the old saying goes, let's wait and see; we might be surprised."

Garcia looked over at his partner, a look of admiration in his eyes. He asked, "Beth, I'm beginning to believe that all detectives should have some training in psychology; we have certainly have had to employ a lot of it in this case, with much of it coming from you. If you ever decide to give up police work, I would bet that you could make a healthy living as a psychological therapist."

Reed laughed, and said, "More likely, I would probably starve to death."

THIRTY

Miss Marly Brooks was sitting in the lone porch chair reading a book when she heard the car drive up. The detective team walked toward her home, and was almost on her first porch step before she closed her book and put it down on the floor of the porch; a look of displeasure on her face. She then rose as the detectives mounted the few remaining steps to her porch; it was obvious to Reed and Garcia that she was not happy to see them again, and she voiced her annoyance in unmistakable terms. "My God, when are you going to start leaving me <u>alone</u>!" She did not expect an answer to her rhetorical question, but continued her objection to the unexpected visit. "I've told you everything that I know about Dr. Carnes. I've admitted that I'm glad that he's dead; too bad it didn't happen sooner. Now what the devil more do you want?!"

The two detectives stood uncomfortably on the small steps in front of the porch, aware that Brooks' frame of mind did not indicate that they would be invited into her home. Detective Reed apologetically replied, "We're sorry to bother you again, Miss Brooks, but we have examined your records at the Chase bank, and have found that you have been credited with regular monthly cash deposits of $400.00. The bank has no record of the source of those funds, and have assumed they were deposited by an anonymous person. Perhaps it is all open and above board, and it may be merely a personal matter, but the fact that you never mentioned that odd financial benefit poses a question for us in terms of whether it might somehow be connected to the murder of Dr. Carnes. Apparently you have been receiving those monthly credits for several years. Would you like to tell us the source of those funds, and why you did not mention those transactions during our previous visits?"

"Of course I would rather not," Brook responded, taken aback by the unexpected question. "I don't really see why that should be any of your business, and I certainly can't see why that information will be of any benefit to you in solving the murder of Dr. Carnes. To be perfectly frank with you, the person that has been generous to me has asked that I not reveal his name; there, you have it," she said indignantly. Now you know that it is a man. He is a friend. What difference does it make whether you know his name or not? It seems stupid to me for you to be spending time on my money problems. I see no reason for you to bring him into your investigation, none at all."

Detective Garcia interjected himself into the questioning with a reply to Brooks. "As I believe we have said before Miss Brooks, in a murder investigation we must follow all sorts of leads and ask all kinds of questions, and we cannot be distracted by trying to answer various questions of those posed by people we are interrogating. Sometimes it puts us into an embarrassing situation, but it is part of our job and has to be done. If you think about it, you have to know that one way or another we will learn the identity of your benefactor, if that is what he is." Marly Brooks looked at the detective as though she did not believe him, and her reluctance to reveal the donor's name showed in her unhappy face.

Beth Reed thought she could convince Brooks to cooperate by letting her know that the bank was being cooperative in helping to identify the man. "Don't you see, Marly, that one or more of the tellers who handled those deposits over the last several years is very likely able to recognize him in a line-up, or we will be able to get his picture from one of the banks security cameras; sooner or later he will definitely be identified. By withholding that information from us now you're merely delaying our ability to solve this murder case. Whether we know the man's name or not, there may be no connection with the murder of Dr. Carnes; but it is just one more item that we need to get out of the way so we can proceed with the investigation in a productive way, and find the killer." Reed paused, to see what kind of reaction she was to get from Brooks, who appeared to be mentally assessing Reed's comments.

Marly Brooks returned to her chair and sat down; she was disconsolate and unquestionably troubled by what she knew she must do. The two detectives were conscious of her state of mind and stood patiently on the stairs, permitting her the time necessary to come to grips with her response. The tic, or whatever it was that made her head twist back and forth seemed worse than ever before. It was obvious that she was struggling to contain herself. She was finally able to calm herself down, looked up as best she could, and spoke in a timid, almost secretive voice. "My neighbor, Charles Bingham, has been my friend since a year or two after his wife died. We have been close, but we have kept it a secret; he has dinner with me every Friday or Saturday night. We never go out to eat, mostly because of me; I'm uncomfortable in public, as you might guess. He doesn't have any children or other family as far as I know. He has a modest pension from the U.S. Postal Service, which he retired from about five years ago, around the time that his wife died. She had a sudden heart attack, he was devastated for quite awhile. I knew his wife; she was a lovely person and we had become friendlier as time went by before she died. Charles began to talk to me a little more a few months after she passed, and I finally felt comfortable enough with him that I invited him for lunch one day. He knew that I had little income, and we talked about what he might be able to do.

It was not long after that when, I think, that he started making those deposits to my account. I believe that was about four years ago; he told me it was to help pay for the dinners I fixed and because he wanted me to spend some money on myself and for little things around the house. Sometimes we have watched television together; we have become very close. I feel terrible about having to break my promise about keeping our relationship concealed. I imagine that trying to keep it secret was hopeless anyway, some other neighbor was bound to find out, if they haven't already. He is a nice man; he has been good to me, but unfortunately his health is not as good as it once was. He won't tell me just how serious his condition is, but I know that he has lost quite a bit of weight recently, and his energy level is way down from what it used to be. I asked him once if he had any other relatives that could be of help to him; I knew a long time ago that he did not have any children of his own. He said that he had a stepson, but he wanted nothing to do with him. I never brought up the subject again. What else can I tell you?"

The detectives looked at each other, both surprised at the revelations, yet realizing that it might all be just another dead end in terms of solving the murder of Dr. Carnes. Detective Reed acknowledged the "confession" of Marly Brooks, "Thank you, Marly, for saving us any further work in getting the name of your benefactor. What you have told us is all more or less personal information, and as the facts appear now, you may never be publicized or need to be brought up in court. As to the personal relationship that you have with Mr. Bingham, unless something further develops that requires it, we have no necessity to inform anyone of that association. We will, of course, be questioning Mr. Bingham, and if we are satisfied that there is no connection to the murder of Dr. Carnes, we can take both of your names out of our file."

"I would really like to have that happen," Brooks replied, "but will you please go easy on Charles; I'm not sure about his heart. He has been the best thing that has happened to me in the last four years; I'd hate to lose him. I really don't know why you have to bother him," she almost pleaded.

"We understand, Miss Brooks, and we appreciate your helping us to clarify the questions about your finances. Do you know if he is home now? We would like to go there when we leave here and settle our involvement with both of you as quickly as we can." Both Reed and Garcia waited for a moment while Brooks reflected on what she had just done, but she then answered Reed's question in a timid voice.

"Yes, I'm sure that he is home," she replied, "but now I am feeling guilty because I have ruined our relationship by telling you his name, and that he is the one who has made those cash deposits to my account. Is it necessary that you tell him that I made those admissions?" The worried look on her face and the hesitation in her voice clearly reflected her concern about their relationship. "I don't know what I would do without him; he is more than just a friend . . . he is my life." Tears came to her eyes as she looked into the faces of the two detectives for signs of sympathy and understanding.

Detective Beth Reed gave Brooks some assurance that it may not be necessary to tell Mr. Bingham of how they learned of his involvement with those cash transactions. "At least for the moment," Detective Reed began to explain, "We will merely tell him that we were able to get his identity through our discussions at the bank. There will be no need to tell him the details of our discussion; if he is home, I'm sure he knows we have been here. As I said before, at a later time we will probably have one of the tellers confirm him as being the person making the deposits through a line-up or a simple face-to-face confrontation, and only if for some reason we find it necessary to do so."

"Well," Miss Brooks said, "Will you please let me know if everything is alright, or if there is some other problem? I am more than anxious to get this all settled." She was remorseful on the one hand, and surprisingly eager to help the detectives in putting an end to her, and her neighbor's involvement in the murder investigation.

"I promise to call you as soon as I can, Miss Brooks, or Detective Garcia will, but right now we want to call on your neighbor. We appreciate the time and information you have given us." Reed started down the few steps and Detective Garcia followed, merely waving his hand in Marly's direction, as she nodded in return.

THIRTY ONE

Detective Garcia had decided not to move their car to the street area in front of Bingham's house, but still asked his "boss" if she minded if they just walked next door.

Reed nodded in agreement, and said, "Of course not, I need the exercise; in fact so do you," she grinned at her partner . . . so they strolled over to Brooks' neighbor. This time Mr. Bingham was not outside sweeping his sidewalk, suggesting to the detectives that he may not have been aware of their visit to Marly Brooks' home. They both thought that Miss Brooks might have been wrong when she said she thought for sure that he was at home; there were no signs of life to be seen from the walkway. They had previously seen his car parked in the ribbon driveway; there was no garage. The car was parked in the driveway as it had been before, so they expected to find him at home. However, after what Marly Brooks had said about Bingham's health, they wondered if they would find him in a state of health that would not permit him to be questioned. Reed voiced their mutual concern: "We may have to call and set up a meeting, or at least find out whether he is all right to meet with us, unless he is at home now and can come to the door. Ring the doorbell, Bob, and let's see what happens. If he doesn't answer, then we'll give him a call."

Detective Garcia pushed the little doorbell and could hear it chime inside, but Bingham did not come to open the door until the detective pushed the bell again. When he did appear, he seemed like a different person to both Reed and Garcia from what they recalled had been his physical condition. Although it had not been a long time since they had seen him last, he appeared to have lost some weight, and his face was more drawn than they had remembered. He was, nevertheless, quite cordial and invited them into his home. He led them to a small living room and waved them toward two matching covered chairs. "Please be seated," he said, waving them toward two stuffed armchairs. "I'm sorry I didn't get to the door quicker; I was back in the kitchen fixing myself some hot tea. As you probably noticed, I'm not all that well anymore, and I can't move as fast as I used to." With some difficulty, he eased himself into an area on the end of the sofa across from the chairs.

Detective Reed responded with some understanding words: "No problem, Mr. Bingham; your neighbor, Miss Brooks, did tell us that your health has deteriorated in recent months. We apologize for not calling to set up an appointment to meet with you. However, we're glad you are home and if you don't mind, we have some more questions to ask you. If you don't feel well enough to talk, please feel free to say so."

"No, I can talk; as long as I can sit, and I can take my time in answering your questions, I should be okay." Charles Bingham sensed that they had learned that he and Marly Brooks had become close friends, and he thought that they wanted to explore that point more with him, but he was confused as to why they would want to do that in the first place.

The detectives had recognized he was an intelligent man during their first meeting, when they encountered him sweeping his walkway. Although he was somewhat physically impaired, it was obvious to the detectives he was still mentally very alert. He was frank about what he thought the detectives wished to discuss, and said, with some hesitation: "Well I know that you just came over from Marly's place; I saw you drive up, and I know that you were there quite awhile. I suppose you want to know more about our relationship, but I don't see how that is going to help you with your murder case, and I'm sure that Marly doesn't see how either." He stopped and coughed a little, putting a handkerchief to his mouth; his eyes became a little watery. Putting the handkerchief back in his pocket, he regained his composure and said, "So what questions do you have in mind?

Senior Detective Reed answered Bingham's question with a statement about the investigation of Miss Brooks' account at the Chase Bank, and what information was revealed. "We have learned about the monthly cash deposits to Brooks' account that you have made for several years, Mr. Bingham. We know you have attempted to remain anonymous in this regard, for whatever reasons, but the bank has been very cooperative in helping us learn your identity. I'm sure you know most banks have security cameras at work inside the facility during banking hours, and most good tellers remember the faces of those depositors who visit the bank with some regularity. We recognize this has all of the appearances of being nothing more than a personal matter, but we must assure ourselves there is no connection with the murder investigation that we are conducting. If you will, do you want to further confirm for us you are, indeed, the individual who has made those $400 cash deposits every month for the past several years?"

Mr. Bingham let out a long sigh, took another brief moment to wipe his nose, hesitated, and then, in a soft voice with obvious distress, he replied. "I guess I always knew at some point that information would come out, but I was hoping it might not be until after I died. Yes, I've been making those deposits for the last three years or more. I didn't start until about a year after my wife died; which was about the time that Marly and I started to develop a relationship; one that has helped us both to survive with some kind of life. I still don't see how that information will help you though; does it?"

"We're not sure at this time, Mr. Bingham; in any event, if we could answer that question we could not reveal it to you anyway; perhaps later," Detective Garcia stated. He then asked, "Why did you feel it necessary to be anonymous? Miss Brooks apparently knew you were her benefactor from the very beginning; is that right?"

"Yes, of course she knew," Bingham answered, "Because I told her what I was going to do, and why, even before I made the first deposit. Although Virginia and I had been married quite a long time, I was my wife's second husband. We were too old at that time to have any children between us, but she had a son that was a neer-do-well, a real trouble maker, and I thought that if he knew about it he would try to cause me some kind of a problem; maybe try to get to be my guardian, or have me committed, just to get his hands on whatever money I did have . . . which is not all that much. When I married Virginia, she had a fair bit of money from her first husband, and I think that her son had his eyes on whatever he might get when she died. She didn't have anything to do with her son for years; she didn't want to; he was pure trouble. I'm grateful that he doesn't have a place in Florida; he lives in New Orleans, a place that fits his personality . . . fast and loose. He got fooled though, because we had a joint Trust, under which he has to wait until I go, which unfortunately might be pretty soon. Marly doesn't know it, but to avoid any problems with my step-son, I've arranged to have him get half of what is left; the other half will go to Miss Brooks. I wanted to set it up so that she would get all of it, but my lawyer said that that arrangement would probably not hold up it court if it was challenged." Bingham was breathing a bit hard and began to shake a little. The long discourse had exhausted him; he wiped his watery eyes again, closing them for a moment.

Reed gave the man a moment to recover his breath and his composure, then inquired: "Well that seems like a logical reason, but you must know what our next question would be; why? Why would you be so generous as to donate $400 every month to a neighbor? You have to know that such action strikes us as being very strange, and now you have informed us that you will leave half of your estate to Marly Brooks? Again, a very unusual situation. However, this information appears to be all of a personal nature, and on the face of it may be of no value at all in solving the killing of Dr. Carnes. Is that correct? Or are we missing something?"

Bingham had settled down, was breathing a bit more normally, yet gave out an audible sigh, one that indicated to the detectives that he was possibly resigning himself to "tell all." "Yes, you have it right, and I agree that it is all very unusual. Virginia and I liked Marly and felt very sorry for her, and we both hated Dr. Carnes for what he had done to her, even though neither of us had ever met him. Our income was modest, so we couldn't do much for her financially when we were both living. I began to visit with Marly about a year after I lost Virginia. I had retired early from the Post Office a few years before that and kept busy making repairs and some improvements around the house. I played a little golf, watched sports on TV, and read a few books, but when I was alone after I lost Virginia, I really didn't know what to do with myself. I started helping Marly with little jobs around her little house, and then we would fix dinner together once in awhile for just the two of us. It became a regular thing; sometimes I would stay late and we would watch television together. She really is a nice person, and I got used to her tic and off-angle head. At one time she fell asleep on my shoulder while watching TV; it felt good. When she awoke her lips were right in front of me, we looked at each other and then we kissed. She is a several years younger than I am, but we both needed each other. I had reached the point in my own life that I realized that life without love is no life at all. We became intimate, promising to keep our activities discreet; we wanted to avoid any difficulties from my stepson or anyone else. We were successful, up until now." He was breathing heavily when he finished, and fished a handkerchief out of his pocket to wipe his eyes.

Just as Charles Bingham completed his tale, Detective Reed's cell phone buzzed; she excused herself and went into another room and closed the door. The caller was Chief Detective Hobson, who first asked Reed where they were and what they were doing. She told him everything, briefly, that had been covered and revealed during the meetings with both Brooks and Bingham. Hobson said, "That is extremely interesting, particularly because it may all fit together with some important information that I just received from the Lab folks, a final and complete report on the blood work and the DNA numbers. As I thought that it would, blood appears to be immerging as the most important factor in solving the murder of Dr. Carnes, which seems to be on the brink of being concluded. I think that the Lab report will get you and Garcia excited, especially since you may finally get off of this case; we need you both on other cases. It is surprisingly coincidental that you happen to be with Mr. Charles Bingham; I want you to bring him in. It appears that Bingham is more than just a party of interest, unless another twist comes up that we don't know about. In any event, as of this moment, the interrogation of Mr. Bingham in my office may unravel this knotty case, unless we discover some flaw in our thinking. It should be interesting, and hopefully revealing, to hear Mr. Bingham's responses to a few questions we have." Detective Reed was surprised at Hobson's comments, yet she was inclined to think that his implied remarks fitted in with what she had started to wonder about in terms of Charles Bingham's involvement with the murder of Dr. Carnes, but she was still at a loss when attempting to define a motive, that is, if he was found to actually be the murderer. She had a flash thought that bringing Bingham into headquarters was going to be an exercise in futility. His story just didn't seem to make any sense, but maybe there was some kind of connection still to be established with the actual killer.

"I don't think that I mentioned Bingham's health, Chief," Reed stated, "It is a bit tenuous at the moment, in my opinion. We'll bring him in, as you have asked, but if it looks like there will be a delay because of his physical condition, I'll call you back in a few minutes; okay?"

"That's fine, Reed," the chief agreed. "Do you think that he will require some kind of special transport? He doesn't have a contagious disease, does he?" Hobson inquired. "If you think that he might be, or if you think that his life is in danger, maybe you should take him straight to a hospital instead of coming in here; we're not equipped to cope with sick people, physically or mentally."

"No, no; I don't think that it is anything all that serious to worry about, chief," Reed assured him. "Garcia and I believe that it is something internal; maybe cancer or a painful ulcer; he is on some kind of medication. I'm sure that we can bring him in; it's just that it may take a few more minutes to get him to understand that that is what we have to do, and to calm him down. He seems to come in and out of mild hyperventilation. The man is somewhat frail, but it is also his mental condition that is unstable at the moment. He has made some admissions that have been obviously very disturbing for him. None-the-less, unless I call you back very soon, we will be there in about half an hour."

Reed clicked off her phone and returned to the room where Garcia and Bingham were passing the time quietly talking about the weather, with Garcia doing most of the talking. Detective Reed wasn't sure about how to inform them of Hobson's request; she faced sort of an awkward situation, and wished that she could first tell Garcia without having Bingham hear the order, concerned about how he would react to the news. She finally bit the bullet and let them know, and as she expected, both men were surprised at Hobson's request and Reed almost felt embarrassed because she could not give them a good justification for bringing Bingham into headquarters, and told them that she didn't know anymore about the request than what she had informed them of. Bingham had already been exhibiting some depression, and the news worsened his feelings; his head was lowered almost to his chest, but he finally resigned himself to the order, and offered no objections to the action; he was almost unconscious of what was going on, almost as if he really didn't care. Nothing more was said and the trio was in the car and on their way in minutes after Bingham got his wallet and a sweater. The fresh air was pleasantly cool, and yet Mr. Bingham was perspiring, even though he had put on his sweater. He sat down in the back of the car, leaned back and closed his eyes, which gave Detective Reed the opportunity to whisper just a bit of the details of her conversation with Chief Detective Hobson to her partner. Garcia silently nodded back to her, and gave her right hand a warm squeeze. The rest of the ride to headquarters was uneventful, with Charles Bingham dozing the whole way, but fitfully. Detective Reed contemplated the possible conclusion of the homicide case, while Detective Garcia was a bit confused over what was happening, and what was going to happen when they met with Chief Detective Hobson.

THIRTY TWO

Cindy, the department's receptionist stopped them as they entered the office. "Hi you two, haven't seen you for awhile." she greeted them. "Chief Hobson asked me to have you take Mr. Bingham into conference room number one. I'm to call and let him know that you have arrived. The coffee station has been refreshed there, so you can help yourselves and Mr. Bingham if he gets hung up with a phone call or something. You can go in right now, and I'll call the chief and let him know that you have arrived with Mr. Bingham."

"Thanks, Cindy," Detective Reed acknowledged, "I don't suppose that you know if anyone else is joining us, do you?"

"Well I do know that there has been a buzz around here this morning involving the Lab staff, so it's possible that they may have someone from that department attend the conference. I'm only guessing," Cindy answered.

"Okay; we'll go on in and get settled," Reed said, as she proceeded ahead of Garcia and Bingham toward the conference room number one.

Charles Bingham had been very quiet during the ride to headquarters, asleep most of the time, but now was more awake and showed signs of agitation at being brought in without being given any reason for the act. "You still haven't told me why you have brought me in here," he said with a nervous, shaky voice. "You can see I'm not feeling well. I need some water; I have to take a pill." He had the look of a cornered scared mouse.

The coffee station also provided a pitcher of water and paper cups, so Bob Garcia poured a glass and handed it to Mr. Bingham, who had a pill in his hand, which he quickly swallowed with the water, then handed the cup back to Detective Garcia. Reed and Garcia looked at each other, both being bothered by the fact that they, too, were not really sure of exactly why Hobson had them bring in Bingham, or what was the point of the conference. Detective Reed had had no opportune time alone with her partner to explain in detail what she believed Hobson had implied, so Garcia was more confused than Beth Reed. His detective mind, however, gave him the thought that Bingham might, just might have somehow been involved in the murder of Dr. Carnes, in some way. He could look at this pathetic individual and could not think of him in any way as being able to kill anyone . . . but then . . . ? Could it be just another detour on the way towards solving the murder of Dr. Carnes?

Detective Reed spoke to Mr. Bingham, concerned that he might collapse; he was quite pale, and shaky. "As soon as our boss gets here, Mr. Bingham, which should be at any moment, we expect to have an answer to your question. At this moment neither Detective Garcia or I know exactly why we were requested to bring you in. We're just as much in the dark as you are. Move to another chair if that one isn't comfortable for you, relax, and have a cup of coffee. I don't think that we will have to wait very long. As a matter of fact, I think that I heard Chief Hobson's voice just now."

As he entered the room, the chief directed his comments to his detective team with a nod, he said, "I'm glad you were able to get here quickly, and apparently with no problems." Hobson had entered the room with another person, whom he did not immediately introduce, but instead walked directly to Mr. Bingham and introduced himself. "I am Chief Detective Clyde Hobson," he said as he reached down to shake Bingham's hand. "And I presume that you are Charles Bingham, neighbor to Miss Marly Brooks, is that correct?"

Bingham started to rise, but then sat back down; the movement showed that his body-strength was at a very low level. "Yes, I am," he replied weakly, offering up a limp right hand, and looking up at the chief with obvious apprehension in his eyes.

The chief turned to the detective team and said, "You both, of course, know Jim Curtis from the Lab department." Reed and Garcia both answered in the affirmative and nodded toward Curtis; then Hobson introduced Curtis to Mr. Bingham. Turning his attention again to the detective team, he said, "Before I get to the reasons for bringing Mr. Bingham here, I would like to have you two recap your interview with Mr. Bingham. And sir," he nodded toward Bingham, "If there is anything you hear that is incorrect, or if you wish to make any statement when they are finished, we will give you ample time to do so. I should also inform you we have activated our recording system for this interrogation so that everything anyone here says will be a matter of record." Bingham sat quietly and gave no response to Hobson's comments; he stared at the chief with vacant eyes. None of the officials were sure that he understood what had been said by the chief.

Reed and Garcia took turns in reporting the questioning of Bingham at his home, and repeated his responses, word for word. They also included the discussion that they had had prior to that, with Marly Brooks. They made it clear that there was no major discrepancy between what Brooks had told them versus Bingham's statements. Detective Reed asked Chief Hobson if he had any questions about the report; he had none. Then she looked at Charles Bingham and asked, "Have you heard everything that Detective Garcia and I have reported, and is what we have reported correct, in your opinion, Mr. Bingham?"

Without any emotion, and without even looking up, he responded with a timid, "I guess so." He sat half hunched over, appearing as though he might fall over at any moment, breathing with some difficulty.

"Alright then," Chief Hobson stated, "I believe it is time to hear from Mr. Curtis; so Jim, would you please inform us as to what your staff has learned; just give us the most significant facts, the ones we have discussed and which are critical to resolving this case. Your report is primarily for the benefit of Detectives Reed and Garcia, and of course for Mr. Bingham to hear."

"Certainly, Chief," Curtis replied, "but for the record, I would like to say first that the Lab staff put in a lot of hours on the examination, accumulation, and comparison of the many blood samples provided, and that we were able to extract enough material from every sample to permit us to generate DNA numbers in every instance. We cannot confirm that each and every piece of clothing that may have contained droplets of blood was found; however, what pieces we did receive were more than ample to substantiate the facts that we established. We know some of the pieces of clothing were likely washed, sent to the cleaners, or disposed of. However, those from which we obtained meaningful information have been retained as evidence, which was with your approval, of course. DNA numbers were also determined from each and every saliva test that was obtained. Now there were two very significant determinations made. The first was that there were some minute drops of blood on the victim's body that were analyzed and found to be the blood type of another person, not of Dr. Carnes; there were also, as expected, some blood on his clothes that was from his own body. The presumption at that point was that the non-Carnes' blood was undoubtedly from the killer. The second significant determination is what I called you about just a little while ago. It was generated by a small amount of dried blood that came from a shoe which we had postponed examining while we checked other items, because it seemed to be the least likely area for us to find blood. But we did. It came from a right shoe that was part of the clothing taken from the premises of Mr. Bingham, under a Court Order, of course."

Curtis looked at Mr. Bingham as he made that statement, and Bingham let out a loud sigh, as though letting all of the air out of his body; his face was a gray ashen color. Jim Curtis continued his report. "Because the shoe was black, the blood had dried to the point that it had blended into the black color, but it also preserved a larger amount of blood because it didn't get absorbed like the blood on fabrics would have. At that point we had an exact match between the blood from the victim's body, and the blood from Mr. Bingham's shoe. Simply stated, both blood spots were confirmed as being from Dr. Richard Carnes. Although we knew that that discovery in itself would be sufficient evidence, I believe, to convict Mr. Bingham, a match was also established with the blood on the doctor's body that was not his with the blood samples taken from Mr. Bingham. That brought us to the conclusion that the killer had to have nicked himself somehow during the stabbing of the victim."

As Curtis concluded his report, Detectives Reed and Garcia were almost in shock; they could not believe that Bingham was the killer of Dr. Carnes, and they felt that all of the work that they had put in on the case just boiled down to simple lab-generated blood evidence, just as Chief Detective Clyde Hobson had believed early on in the homicide.

In some respects it was a let-down for them, yet at the same time they felt good that it appeared that the case was finally solved. Everyone in the room was quiet for awhile, except Bingham, who sat there whimpering a little with a white-sheet face, repeating "Oh God, Oh God." until Chief Hobson spoke.

"Thank you, Jim; I'll talk to you a little later about protecting the evidence you have so well provided for us, and we will probably get together with someone from the prosecutor's office tomorrow morning to establish how this should all play out in court. You may leave now, Jim, with thanks from all of us; you and your staff have done a great job." He shook Jim's hand, as did Reed and Garcia, each congratulating him on a job well done. Curtis left with a small satisfying smile on his face.

Chief Hobson turned and faced Mr. Bingham, who sat with his head down, as though he was staring at a spot on the floor. Tears were flowing down his pale cheeks and a slight whimpering sound came from somewhere inside his body. "Mr. Bingham," Hobson said loudly, hoping to rouse the man to pay attention. Bingham slowly raised his head, but said nothing. "You have heard the evidence against you," the chief continued, "and your reaction would indicate that you are not disputing what you have heard, so you must know now that you are technically under arrest for the murder of Dr. Carnes. If you can, would you please tell us what motivated you to kill Dr. Carnes, which obviously you now cannot deny." Trembling, and with great hesitation, Bingham's weak voice began to tell the tale.

Speaking slowly, and with some hesitation, Bingham replied to Chief Hobson's request. "You all know what happened to Marly, but none of you could possibly know the suffering she has had to endure and the loneliness she has had." Bingham stopped, brought out a handkerchief and dabbed at his eyes. "Lord I saw it for so many years; she had pain, too, but she had no one to complain to . . . until the time I came into her life." Bingham paused, tried to take a deep breath, but could not; he coughed a bit, and for a moment looked as if he could not continue. However, he braced himself and went on with what happened. "I hated that doctor, even though I had never met him. There was never a question in Marly's mind as to what happened to her as a consequence of being treated by Dr. Carnes, and I know that she has been totally truthful; I know her mind. Whether or not she had had the opportunity to prove her claim in court is beside the point. He undoubtedly knew that she didn't have the money to hire a good attorney, so he wasn't concerned about her problem, or being able to bring suit against him. He probably could have had her file a claim under his insurance coverage for some reasonable amount, or he could have just given her some financial aid. No; he did nothing. Not with therapy, money, or whatever. He took the easy way out; he ignored her. He was wealthy enough; and I understood that he was always trying to make more big bucks by getting into various investments, and Marly learned somehow that he also was a heavy gambler. Marly and I talked about him every so often; we couldn't avoid the subject." Bingham paused, gasped a little for breath, and asked for a glass of water. When it was given to him he took another little pill out of a box from his pocket, and swallowed it with another glass of water that Detective Garcia had handed him. Everyone just waited to see if he would be able to continue.

Chief Hobson asked, "Are you able to go on, Mr. Bingham, or do you need to rest a little longer?"

Bingham let out a loud sigh and said, "No, I better go on so you can get the whole story before I die." It was not intended to be a joke . . . one could see that in his eyes. "A few months ago I was diagnosed with incurable pancreatic cancer. It had advanced to the point that nothing could be done, and I was told that I had only months to live, if that. I decided what I wanted to do. Marly and I were a couple, in every way, but I did not want her to know what I planned or to be involved. My life was really over." Bingham coughed and wiped his eyes again, his hands shook as though he had Parkinson's disease.

"I did it, I stabbed the bastard right in the heart; I had to do it while I still had the strength. I did it for Marly, but I did it for myself too. I just couldn't accept the possibility that he could go on enjoying life, while Marly continued with her lousy life. She will get a chunk of the money I have left, and my hope is that she will find someone else to make her life a bit more pleasant. There, you have it. Don't ask me if I want a lawyer; I don't think that I'll need one; won't be around long enough. Are you going to let me go home now?"

Detective Reed replied, "We'll have to talk to the Prosecutor about that, Mr. Bingham, which we will do shortly. Just two more questions Mr. Bingham. The first is, did you wear a hat or cap the evening of the murder, and if so, what kind was it?"

"Yes, I did wear a cap that night, an Irish Tam. That is one of the ways Marly passes the time; she enjoys her knitting; she knitted several sweaters for me, and the green Tam. I know that my monthly money has helped her buy the yarns and stuff." Bingham coughed, put his handkerchief to his teary eyes, and in a whisper said, "She is truly a wonderful and caring person." He paused, looked blankly at the detectives, and then remembered about Detective Reed's comment about having two questions, and he started to ask her about what her second question was, but Detective Reed spoke first. "We have a general description of the knife you used, Mr. Bingham, but we do not have the knife. What kind was it, and do you still have it?"

Bingham looked at Reed as though surprised by the question, then raised his head a bit, giving an indication that he understood the question, and mumbled an answer. "The knife, oh, the knife. Yes, yes, I still have it; it is an antique knife that my wife bought years ago at an antique shop; it is quite sturdy. Virginia used to go to the Auld Lang Syne shop; she got a lot of bargains there." The detectives looked spooked by that comment, but Bingham went on to answer the question. "I keep it among my tools, it comes in handy quite often. If you want it, you can have it; it's in my kitchen work tools' drawer."

Detective Garcia said, "I'm sorry, Mr. Bingham, there is one more question that we need an answer to in order to satisfy my curiosity, which was brought on by Mr. Curtis' report. Did you nick yourself during the stabbing of Dr. Carnes? Curtis reported that they found a drop of your blood on the victim's body."

Bingham looked confused for a moment, and then replied, almost sheepishly. "I guess I did. I had some blood on my hand when I got home, but I thought that it was from Dr. Carnes, but then I saw some blood on my one finger; I must have gripped the knife awkwardly when I pulled it out of his body. It's all healed up."

Chief Detective Clyde Hobson, Detective Beth Reed and Detective Robert Garcia sat in awe of the man in front of them, a man who appeared to be weak and dying, yet who had had the fortitude to execute a person he believed had caused the person he loved to suffer a life of discomfort and isolation. The interrogation resulted in the conclusion of a murder case than none of them would ever forget.

The case never made it to court; Charles Bingham died before he could be brought to trial.

EPILOGUE

After the case of the murder of Dr. Richard Carnes was solved, Detectives Beth Reed and Bob Garcia were assigned to another homicide case, but they were both uncomfortable in the knowledge that their personal involvement with each other violated the police department's code of conduct for members of the force. They presented themselves together to Chief Detective Clyde Hobson, and informed him of their decision to leave the department and seek employment elsewhere. They then explained their reasons, and the chief acknowledged that he had been aware of their association toward the end of the Carne's case, but he did not want to take any action until the case was closed. He accepted their resignations, wishing them good luck in whatever future career changes that they might make, and also in their personal lives.

The team contacted Officer Andrew Nichols of the Jacksonville Police Department, and made an appointment to meet him to discuss their employment plans. As it developed, Officer Nichols had started to set up a personal security systems company, with the intention of leaving the Jacksonville force himself; he invited Reed and Garcia to join him, if they wished. They joined with the now Mr. Nichols, and together they were very successful in their new careers. One year exactly, from the date of the murder of Dr. Richard Carnes, Beth Reed and Bob Garcia were married.

Both Zach Segal and Sam Meyers were convicted of attempting to defraud Mrs. Elizabeth Gordon and were sentenced to two years in prison and five years of probation. The Auld Lang Syne antique shop was closed.

Mr. Roland LeBland continued with his commercial real estate marketing business, and in a strange twist of things, employed Justin Douglas to perform whatever legal work was required.

Chief Detective Clyde Hobson remained in his position with the Orange Grove Police Department until he took early retirement; he stayed in the community he had served for over thirty years . . . spending his time golfing and fishing.

Mrs. Opal Carnes sold her home, and embarked on a series of cruise ship journeys to various islands in the Atlantic; she settled in San Juan, Puerto Rico with a planter, but never married again. Beth Reed never got that antique chair.

Miss Marly Brooks was devastated by the death of Charles Bingham, but her future was brightened considerably with the receipt of half of the assets he had held at the time of his death. The money was sufficient to allow her to seek the services of the best neurological surgeon in Florida, which resulted in her having almost a full recovery of the normal movement of her neck and head. She moved into a small condo near the hospital where she had been treated, became a nurse's assistant, and was popular with several of the male nurses.